Praise for Ril

"With poise and restraint, Rilla Askew's his   ae
brilliant, multifaceted story of an intelligent, virtuous, and indomitable woman."

—*Foreword Reviews*

"Rilla Askew—a storyteller of truth and grace in all she writes, whether novel or essay—moves us to compassionately consider Oklahoma in all its faces. Oklahoma's is a rough story of theft and coercion, of beauty and tenderness. In *Most American*, Askew teaches us to see with wiser eyes."

—U.S. Poet Laureate Joy Harjo

"Askew's unflinching portrait of a family whipsawed from within and without is a story for our time. It's proof of Askew's flat out genius that *Kind of Kin* is merciless, yet strangely full of mercy."

—Ben Fountain, Author of National Book Award Finalist *Billy Lynn's Long Halftime Walk*

"Askew's command of language is a pleasure to behold, bringing out the pain and wonder of her story with a bittersweet immediacy."

—*Publishers Weekly*

"Askew's characters are complex, fraught with those concerns, tendencies, and motivations that make us the best and worst of who we are. . . . *Fire in Beulah* touches on the substance of morality and the composition of the human spirit, underscoring the fact that our lives transcend perceived boundaries."

—*Black Issues Book Review*

"Askew artfully lays bare the sins and promises of pioneer society. *The Mercy Seat* is a story of betrayal and revenge. But it is also the story of self-discovery and the possibilities of salvation. Few can deny its relentless, almost hypnotic, force."

—*The New York Times Book Review*

"A triumph of scholarship and imagination . . . a powerful novel in a mesmerizing prose out of the Old Testament by way of Faulkner. Askew is a prodigious talent."

—*New York Newsday*

"Askew orchestrates her many voices with the assurance of a master composer. But although the author's technical skill will take your breath away, it's ultimately her warm heart that makes *Strange Business* a small masterpiece."

—*Washington Post Book World*

Also by Rilla Askew:

Strange Business (1992)
The Mercy Seat (1997)
Fire in Beulah (2001)
Harpsong (2007)
Kind of Kin (2013)
Most American: Notes from a Wounded Place (2017)
Prize for the Fire (2022)

the HUNGRY and the HAUNTED

RILLA ASKEW

the HUNGRY *and the* HAUNTED

STORIES

Fort Smith, Arkansas

THE HUNGRY AND THE HAUNTED:
STORIES

© 2024 by Rilla Askew
All rights reserved

Cover: *Airline Motel sign Oklahoma City, Oklahoma*,
from the John Margolies Roadside America Photograph Archive,
Library of Congress, Prints and Photographs Division.

Publisher's note:
This is a work of fiction. Names, characters, places, and incidents
either are the product of the author's imagination or are used fictitiously,
and any resemblance to actual persons, living or dead, events,
or locales is entirely coincidental.

Portions of "That Grief, That Fury" were first published as "Tahlequah"
in *Nimrod International Journal,* Volume 37 Number 1, Fall/Winter 1993.

"Ritual" was first published in *Saint Katherine Review,* Volume 3 Number 3, 2013.

"Two of Her" was first published in *R&R Literary Magazine* in Spring 2024.

Belle Point Press, LLC
Fort Smith, Arkansas
bellepointpress.com
editor@bellepointpress.com

Find Belle Point Press
on Facebook, Substack,
and Instagram (@bellepointpress)

Printed in the United States of America

28 27 26 25 24   1 2 3 4 5

Library of Congress Control Number: 2024933706

ISBN: 978-1-960215-17-8

HH/BPP35

For the lost ones

Contents

Solstice

1999

We lived on the border then. I mean for real on the border, like, our backyard was in Arkansas and our front porch in Oklahoma. My Uncle Oscar said we were showing our bums to the Old South and our snoots to the New West, and he didn't say it like that was a good thing. He didn't want to be living there. He wanted to go home to Oklahoma.

"Hell, Oscar," my brother Cecil said, "step out to the road yonder, you'll be in Oklahoma." But that wasn't what Oscar meant. He wanted to go home to the house he grew up in, which he couldn't because it got torn down fifty years ago, and even if it was still there, he couldn't live in it alone. He had bad eyes to where he couldn't see what was right in front of him, only circles around a blurry center, so he couldn't drive or shop for himself. He'd had three car wrecks by the time my brothers took the keys away and sold his car and made him come live with us in Arkoma. That was a family decision, same as how they got together and decided I'd live with Cecil after Mama died, because Cecil and Sally's kids were grown and they had the most room. Nobody really wanted to look after Oscar, same as nobody really wanted to look after me, so I sort of took it on as my job to do that. I'd come out to the porch, where he sat most days till it got too hot or too cold, and he'd say, "How you doing this morning, sister?"

"Good," I'd say, and give him his coffee and ask if he wanted oatmeal or toast this morning. He'd pat the plastic porch chair next to him. "Sit awhile, sister. You work too damn hard for a six-year-old."

"I'm nine," I'd say.

"Inverted six," he'd answer, like that made any sense. I'd sit and we'd watch the hummingbirds zoom each other at the feeder and he'd tell stories till it got time for me to go get ready for school. Oscar was my great-uncle, really—him and my grandpa were brothers, but I never knew my grandpa because he died before I was born—and Uncle Oscar never got married, never had any kids. He'd left home at thirteen, he said, and traveled around the country, got in a bunch of fights with scabs and lawmen. I thought a scab was like if you skinned your knee and it healed over, so in my mind I'd see Uncle Oscar fighting these giant crusty scabs like in a cartoon. Kids are so literal sometimes. He told me about the time him and another guy raced a freight train and the other guy slipped and fell under and got his legs cut off. He told me how his one grandpa ran a post office and a sawmill, and his other grandpa got cheated out of a coal mine. Or something like that. I wish I'd listened better. Then one day Uncle Oscar quit talking.

I'd bring him his coffee, but he wouldn't ask how I was doing or say inverted six or any of that anymore. I'd sit in the plastic chair anyway and watch the hummingbirds while he stared across the road at the empty field. I knew he couldn't see it really, on account of his degeneration, but it was like he was studying something out there. I don't remember how long it went on like that. Probably a few weeks. Once or twice, he'd say something like, it's all fixing to change but don't nobody see it. Or he might say: reckon if I started walking? A fella could just start walking, like in the movies. Just walk off into the sunset. But if I said anything back, like, change how? or where do you want to go?, he wouldn't answer. Then one morning—it was

real early, I remember; the sun rising behind the house was making long, long shadows in the yard—Oscar heaved a big sigh with
his eyes closed. "It's time," he said. He opened his eyes and looked
at me. I was just a halo of brown hair around a tan-colored blur to
him—he'd told me that one time—but he smiled in my direction.
"You coming with me, sister?"

"Hell yeah," I said.

He laughed so loud I thought Sally might come out to the porch
to see what we were carrying on about. Then he got quiet. Heaved
that big sigh again. "Tomorrow's the day."

"All right," I said.

"We'll have to be up early. Short night tonight." He folded his lips
tight around his teeth. "Shortest all year."

HE shook me awake before daylight. I gave him the truck key I'd
swiped off Cecil's bureau, and we eased the truck down the driveway
without starting it or turning on the lights. "Sun'll be up before you
know it," he said. And that was a true fact. We'd hardly left town
before it got light enough to see. People were passing us now, on
their way to work. He turned onto the highway toward Pocola, pulled
over, got out and walked to the back of the truck. So I did. The sun
was a burning slice of orange coming up over Fort Smith. He was
staring right at it. "Is that how your eyes got burned out?" I asked
him. "Looking at the sun?"

"No, sister. That's just age and fate." But he was still staring at that
orange ball, which I couldn't. I already had a white spot in front of
me that moved with my eyes no matter where I put them. I stared at
the ground, blinking hard, then turned to look west, where the sky
and mountains were still smoky blue. In a minute, Uncle Oscar got
back in the truck, so I did, and we headed that direction.

I didn't worry then about how he could see to drive. Probably he just followed the outside lines of the road and hoped no cars or deer were in the blurry middle. He turned onto a country road after a while—no pavement, no traffic. The road got smaller and rougher until it was pretty much just a track. He knew right where he was going. I look back now, though, I think it's a miracle we made it all the way to the mounds without a wreck.

Well, not the actual mounds yet, but the outside fence that goes for acres around them. Oscar set the parking brake and got out. So I did. The site didn't look like much, just scrub oak and underbrush every direction. You couldn't see the mounds from where we were. You couldn't even see the fence hardly, so much brush and poison ivy had grown up over it. Uncle Oscar found a fairly cleared spot, pulled a pair of pliers out of his overalls pocket, and cut through the chain-link, *snip, snip, snip, snip*. He stretched open a hole wide enough for me to climb through, then squeezed through after me. We stood in the weeds, squinting. The sun was hot already. The cicadas and grasshoppers were buzzing everywhere. "You're gonna get covered in chiggers," he said. "I'm sorry."

"That's all right," I said. "What are we doing?"

But my uncle just stood with his face turned up to the sky. Then he started walking, making his way through the tangled brush. So I followed.

It wasn't easy. There was no path, briars and brambles caught you, clawed branches crossed in front of you. Oscar had to hold them back so they wouldn't whip me in the face. Afterwhile, we came out in a clearing on the back side of a big grass-thatched hut. He waved me to be still with his hand, his head cocked, listening. All you could hear was crows and insects. He crept out in the clearing. So I did. Then we walked around to the front. The hut was really old; it was built out of dried mud, and the thatched roof came to a peak at the top and hung down off the sides in ragged brown strips. It had a blank open space for a door, no windows.

"Looka there," he said, disgusted.

"What?"

Then I saw the white plastic Wal-Mart sack caught in the dead grass on the roof like a flattened ghost. It must've looked like a white blob to my uncle, but he knew what it was. "Blamed thing blowed all the way here from Poteau."

"Maybe," I said, because I was thinking, everybody uses Wal-Mart sacks. Could've been somebody from Spiro or Pocola threw it out their car window.

"Nothing's sacred anymore." My uncle stood glaring at the roof. "Never was." He walked over to the mud wall, squatted down with his hands clasped in a saddle for me to put my foot there. "Crawl up and get it, sister. I can't stand looking at it."

My uncle had to be like eighty years old, he was built tough and wiry, like me, but still—he was old. I didn't know if he could hold me. I did like he said, though, put my foot in his hands and he boosted me up with a grunt. The sack wasn't stuck too far up, I only had to crawl a little ways, but I could hear the dead grasses crunching under me. They were so aged and dry, I felt like I was breaking them. I thought the ancient ones that built this hut wouldn't appreciate me breaking their roof, and also I was worried about bugs, so I scrabbled up fast, stretched out and got the sack loose, shimmied back down till my legs were hanging off the edge.

"I got you!" Oscar said. I felt his hands grab my hip bones, so I let go. He went *umph!,* then next thing I knew we were both laid out on the ground and my uncle was bleeding bad from a cut between his eyebrows.

"I'm sorry. I'm sorry!" I thought I'd killed him. He was so still, and the blood was just pouring, right out of his forehead, making a red pool on the dirt path. In a minute, he moved and groaned. "Lord ha' mercy," he said. He put his palm up, tried to cup the blood, but it kept coming. I started to cry. "Here now, sister," he said. "Don't do that. I'm all right. Go back to the truck and get me something to hold on this." I shook my head—there was no way I could find the path back through that scrub—but Oscar had his eyes shut and didn't see. I wadded up the Wal-Mart sack and put it in his free hand. He brought it up to cover the other one, held both hands pressed tight to his forehead. That slick plastic didn't help much but it helped some. The blood wasn't gushing now, just oozing out around the sack a little, dripping down. "I'm going to lay here a minute," he said. "You hear anybody coming, you let me know."

"Who'd be coming all the way out here?"

"Tourists."

I looked around. The old ragged-looking hut in the clearing, the dirt path, clotted undergrowth creeping in on all sides. "Why?"

"It's the solstice. People think they're going to see something. I don't reckon they'll come till evening, but you never know."

The sun was burning hot. I was sweating. So was my uncle. I don't know how long he laid there. "Well, missy," he said finally, "here's a fine mess." He was talking about the blood all down his bib overalls, the dark pool on the path. He lowered the wadded sack away from his forehead, sort of tentative like. The blood was a thick blob on the cut but it wasn't streaming now.

"Did my foot do that?" I said.

"No, honey. Not you." He dabbed at the blob real lightly with one finger. "Reckon it'll hold." He tossed the smeared sack off into the brush. "Let's go in." Oscar rolled over onto his hands and knees, grunting, and pushed himself up. I tried to help him, but he batted my hands away. "I got it, I got it!"

Inside the hut wasn't any cooler but at least it was out of the sun. Light streamed in through a big hole at the peak of the roof, making a ragged bright spot on the dirt floor, and there was more daylight coming in through the open door. Otherwise, it was dark, damp, and smelled like a storm cellar. My uncle went to the circle of sunlight, grunted as he got down on the ground. I sat on the dirt floor next to him. I figured it was too late to worry about getting in trouble for dirty britches. Mine were already a filthy mess.

"How old are you, sister?"

"Nine," I said, even though I'd turned ten last month. But it was our ritual. I wanted him to say inverted six but instead he said, "When you get grown, I want you to remember that when you were nine years old, your old Uncle Oscar told you the facts. Don't matter what the rest of them say."

"Yes, sir," I said.

"It was Depression days—you know about the Great Depression?"

I nodded. He'd told me himself, a bunch of times, but my uncle's part-blind eyes weren't on me. He was staring at the sunlight on the floor without blinking, same as he'd stared at the orange ball over Fort Smith.

"Hard times back then. You took any job of work you could get. If you could even get one. I heard this Pocola Mining Company was hiring, I hitched straight out here to see if I could get hired. I wasn't but thirteen, but I was tough and a good talker and a demon with a shovel, and they took me on. They weren't mining coal, see, they were digging for Indian relics—such things sold for a lot, even back then—and that's what these fellows were after. They had a lease to dig in the mounds and keep what they found, which was mostly just broken pots and arrowheads at that point, and a whole lotta dirt. Their lease was fixing to run out, though, and the government was trying to shut them down, and they were getting desperate, so they hired me and a couple of out-of-work coal miners, and we sunk a shaft in that big saddleback mound." He waved his hand at the blank wall like I could see what he was talking about, which of course I couldn't. "Had so many holes in it already, looked like a big round brown Swiss cheese, but—*deeper!* Mr. McKenzie kept saying, *deeper! This here's the place, I feel it in my bones!* Well, you could laugh at that now, if it wasn't so awful. And we kept digging."

He got quiet. I heard a mosquito's whine. Then it was two of them. Then three. I smashed one dead on my arm. "Uncle Oscar," I said.

"I'll never in my life forget it," he murmured. "The day we broke through."

I slapped a mosquito on my neck. "I'm going outside."

No answer. It was like those weeks of him sitting silent on the front porch. So I went out to the sun to escape the mosquitoes, even though it was hot as blue blazes out there. Sun sweltering down. Flies buzzing and crawling all over the dark spot in the path where my uncle bled. I heard voices. I couldn't tell how many, a few grown-ups, a bunch of kids. They were still a ways away, you couldn't see them for the underbrush and how the path turned, but they were headed our direction. I went back to the hut. I couldn't see inside—my eyes were too blinded from the sun.

"You wanted me to let you know if somebody was coming."

I heard him grunt, heard his overalls scrape the dirt. Then he was standing at the door, blinking, looking wan and pale. The cut place was a dark red blob between his eyes, and his freckles and age spots stood out on his white face. He motioned me to come with him. We went around to the back of the hut, stepped under the trees into the underbrush. In a minute we heard kids yelling: *what is it? what is it? eww! look at that!* So we knew they'd found the bloody spot. The main voice was a man's voice. It was just sort of monotonous, droning on and on, telling the grown-ups something. "That's the park ranger,"

my uncle said. "Lies. Pure dee lies. And a few facts." A woman's voice
called out, *Sonny, quit that! Come away from there!* The man's voice
was still talking. In a minute the sound went sort of muffled, like in
a pillowcase or a cave, so I knew they'd went inside the hut.

"Let's go," Oscar said.

I was hoping we'd head back to the truck, but he started walking
toward a hump of hill off a ways in the distance. It wasn't a hill, of
course, or not a natural one—it was one of the mounds, the biggest
I could see then, all covered in brush and scrub, not so thick as in
the lowlands, but thick enough. My uncle started climbing, so I
followed. That mound didn't look like much from below but when
you got to the top you could see for miles in every direction. "Stand
here," he said. He pointed off to the north. I could see the river meandering wide and glinting brown. He pointed south to where the
mountains marched off smoky blue to the horizon. He pointed east,
where it was just green tops of oaks and hickories, and then west,
finally, where the land flattened to yellow prairie. There were more
mounds that direction, another big one and a few others like low
humps on the earth around a big, flat grassy field with the dirt path
meandering along the side of it. The sun was straight up overhead.
My uncle grunted and got down on the ground, so I did the same.
You couldn't see anything now, just sumac and scrub oak all scrabbled
together. The view was hidden from us, and we were hidden from it.

"This ain't the one we want," he said, "but it'll do for now." I could
hear the kids shouting as they passed below, the ranger's voice droning. Oscar shook his head, disgusted. "See, that's what I mean," he
whispered. "Lies and more lies. This ain't the burying mound. Not
the real one. Otherwise, we couldn't sit here."

"Are you getting hungry?" I whispered back, because I sure was,
but my uncle sat frowning, his mouth pursed, till the ranger and
tourists walked on.

"They scraped it down to the nub," Oscar said. "Sifted every particle of soil and clot of clay. Took away every bone and fragment. Then the government brung in a backhoe and built it back up again."

"What for?"

"For tourists to come gawk at. Why else?" He said it the same way he said our bums were to the South and our snoots facing West. "But, it was too late by then. Miners had already done their worst. And not just them, sister. Me too. I was right there with them. Can you keep a secret?"

"Sure I can."

Then he told me the story:

A hot August morning, but it wasn't hot inside the tunnel, he said, because it's always the same temperature inside the earth, any mine or cave. The earth holds its own, he said. Or tries to. Like the grave. They'd been digging for weeks. The mound was dirt, not shale and rock like a coal mine, but that dirt had been packed down for centuries, and they were digging by hand, using picks and shovels, their boss man hollering, *deeper, boys, deeper! This here's the one!*

"And it was, missy. It truly was."

"This mound where we're sitting?"

"This same location. Not this same dirt."

That morning, they came to a solid wall deep inside the mound. It was cedar posts joined together in a big circle to make a room, Oscar said, and hard as limestone. They didn't know that yet, but they knew it was something. Their boss man, Mr. McKenzie, was excited. *Break it down, boys, break on through!* And they went to work with their pickaxes, my uncle and two coal miners. They'd each take a turn swinging at the same place, *whack, whack, whack,* till finally—

"*Sssssss,* oh holy God, you never smelled nothing like it! The stench that come pouring out, Lord God, I can't describe it. Never could." His voice dropped to a whisper. "It was my swing that done it, sister. My last whack with the pickaxe that broke through. And out she poured."

"What poured?"

"Them dead warriors. Them chiefs. Not just their decayed bodies— oh, it was hundreds buried in there—but their *souls*, rushing out in fury. I believe that. I've always believed it. We were all gagging. I was scared. Them coal miners was too. We wanted to quit right then, but Mr. McKenzie wouldn't let us. He didn't care about that smell, didn't care he was disturbing their spirits. He was after their stone pipes and amulets and statues, after anything he thought he could sell. The dead don't go for that, sister. You know that, don't you?"

I thought back to me scrabbling on the grass roof. "You reckon they're mad I was crawling on their roof?"

He blinked at me a second. "Oh. No, hon. That's just a replica. Built by the government. Same as this hill."

"So there's no ghosts there?"

"There's ghosts everywhere." He sat still a minute, staring at nothing. "I been running from 'em all my life, sis. But you can't outrun 'em. No use to try."

I started feeling scared. "Are they going to come up out of the grave?"

"No." He took a big sigh. "No, that ain't it." Then he went on:

The diggers made a big tunnel into the burial chamber, he said, brought in torches, brought in wheelbarrows, started carrying out everything they could grab—engraved shells and breastplates and huge clay pots filled with pearls. "The floor was covered in bones," he said, "laid out on mats, some bare naked, some wearing feathered robes. Or that's how it was when we started, but they scattered the bones every which way, grabbing for loot. You ever see a feeding frenzy?"

"I don't know. Like when Cecil throws pellets on the pond to feed his catfish?"

"Like that. Only worse."

The men walked on top of the bones, tossed them aside, toted them out by the wheelbarrow and dumped them at the tunnel entrance. "Like they were just scrap to put on the trash heap," he said. "No sense of the sacred. And that smell never quit. Every time I went in, I'd have to tie my handkerchief over my nose. Every time I took a load out, I wouldn't look at what I was pushing. If it was just leg bones or something, you could maybe tell yourself it was dead animals and keep going. But you couldn't lie to yourself about human skulls. They had eyeholes in front, had jawbones and teeth. You couldn't lie about human rib cages. Human hands. Human feet."

"What happened to them?"

"Oh, that's the job they put me on. Wouldn't you know. Mr. McKenzie decided them bones was what was stinking up the place, so he had me load them back in the wheelbarrow and tote them to the river. Time and again, a hundred trips at least. No plum job in August, let me tell you. I always used to wonder," he said, touching that wounded place on his forehead, "if I'd stayed inside the mound digging up relics instead of taking bones to the river, would I have got rich? Instead of running all my life? I was just a kid, I couldn't see how snake drawings on conch shells and clay pipes shaped like a woman had any value. But I understood about bones. Every time I tipped that barrow to dump them in the river, I knew what I was doing was wrong."

"You're going to make it bleed again," I said. He'd rubbed the clotted blood away. I could see the cut now.

"What's it look like?" he asked me.

"Like a red *v*."

He traced it with his finger. "An arrowhead?"

I studied it. "Yeah. You could call it that."

He nodded. "We better get over there before that ranger comes back with his tourists."

"Over where?"

"Temple mound. That's the right one for what we want."

"What is it we want?" Truthfully, I didn't want anything except to go back to Cecil's house and cool off and get something to eat.

"I don't know yet." He got to his feet, grunting, and started down the mound. So I followed. We made our way through the scrub, then crossed the big open space on the dirt path till we reached the biggest mound, even bigger than the one we were just on. Another climb, this one even steeper, but the top was cleared, like somebody'd been at it with the brush hog. Oscar went to the exact center and sat down, motioned me over. "Watch yonder," he said, pointing. "Right over that small mound there is where the sun's fixing to set."

I squinted up at the sky. "Not for a while yet."

"When it does, though, I mean."

"All right," I said.

"Listen."

I did, but I didn't hear anything. Even the crows had gone quiet. I looked at my uncle's face—he was listening to something I couldn't hear.

"Is this one a grave, too?" I whispered. I was getting spooked again.

"No, sister. This here's where they had their rites and rituals. It'd be where they talked to God. If you want to put it like that. Which I don't."

"How do you want to put it?"

"None of our business how to put it. None of this place is. They done what they done, and we'd ought to have left it alone."

"What are we doing here then?"

"Choctaws knew. When this was their land, they didn't mess with it. You weren't going to see them digging around in these mounds. Some folks see what's sacred and some absolutely don't." He turned his face to me. "I had to lose my sight before I could see it. Don't let that happen to you, sis."

"Okay," I said. I was hot and sweaty, and hungry, and my chigger bites were itching bad. "Can we go home now?"

"When it's time," he said. "You'll have to talk to that ranger. He's a good enough fella, he'll see you home safe. Just don't listen to how he tells it."

"Tells what?"

"What I'm telling you. They didn't live like kings and pharaohs. That's a white man's way of thinking. They didn't rule over these valleys that way. And I didn't just tote bones to the river. I helped burn their feather robes and baskets and reed mats—they'd started disintegrating as soon as they hit the light and air anyway. Some of the bones did too. I'd go to pick one up, it'd turn to chalk and dust under my hand." He shook his head. His forehead was red with sunburn. That cut v between his eyes was bright ruby red. I felt my face. I was getting burned too.

"Can we at least go in the shade?" I asked, though there was no shade near around.

"This mound here," he said, waving his hand in a circle, "is lined up for the summer solstice. That one yonder," he pointed, "is lined up for winter. They had their rites and rituals, they knew the stars, the sun's movement. Used to be a time when we had our own rituals, but we've forgot 'em. We throwed everything out of balance." He gave one of those big sighs again. Not like he was bored or sad, more like he was trying to suck in his deepest, longest breath. "I helped set the dynamite charge," he said. "After they'd took what they took, sold it to dealers. Looted that grave to the marrow, then blew it to smithereens. And I went right along with them."

"I thought you said they scraped it to the nub."

"That too. We done the looting and the blowing up, archaeologists swooped in later and done the sifting and scraping. I don't see a world of difference."

"Well," I said, "might be some."

"I lit out from home next morning and never come back. Thirteen years old. Riding the rails. Running all over the country. But you can't outrun 'em, sister. Can't never undo what's been done. You can only own it. Come back and take your medicine. You watch yonder for the sun going down. I'm going to sit here a spell and listen."

He went quiet again. The blood on his overalls bib was dried now but a couple of flies were buzzing around it anyway.

"Uncle Oscar?" He was breathing soft and steady, but he didn't move, didn't talk, not through the rest of the afternoon while the cut on his forehead got redder and he was getting more sunburnt. Not when the ranger came leading another group of tourists along the trail near sunset. I heard them a ways off, the ranger's voice droning. The sun was lowering over the smaller mound directly in front of us, just like Oscar said. "Look," I said. But my uncle had already gone where he was going. His eyes were still open, he was still sitting cross-legged on the ground, the flies were still buzzing around his bib overalls, but he wasn't breathing anymore. I touched him on the shoulder. He was hard as stone.

"Don't worry," I whispered. "I can keep a secret."

I got up and went quietly down the back side of the mound and walked around to where the ranger was talking to the tourists. They weren't little kids now but middle-aged couples smelling of mosquito repellent and resting on benches while they listened to the ranger talk. I scared them when I appeared on the path and told them I was lost. I ruined the ranger's talk because I showed up right when the sun was a bright orange ball disappearing over the hump of earth the same way it had risen that morning over Fort Smith. But he was nice. He took me to his office and helped me call my brother and waited with me till Cecil come got me in Sally's car.

I could have told them my uncle was up there, I guess. But what good would that have done? They'd have just gone up and got him and took him someplace and buried him, and he didn't want that. I told them it was all me. I said I woke up and found Uncle Oscar missing and took my brother's truck to go find him and got lost.

Cecil said, "You can't drive a truck, Daphne, you're not but ten years old."

I said, "Well, I thought I could. That's how come me to get stuck."

It took them a week to find the truck. I couldn't describe where we left it. Where *I* left it, I said. Nobody ever found my uncle. At least, I never heard that they did. Somebody would have come told Cecil if they found him, I believe. What I think is, he sat there dead and turned to stone, and that's why nobody found him. He didn't smell like anything. He just looked like part of the earth. That's the secret he wanted me to keep. Not what he did when he was thirteen years old, but how he ended it, how he came back and tried to join them, how he'd quit running from ghosts. If anybody had wanted him, they would have looked harder to find him. That's what I think.

Two of Her

1975

There had always been two of her, inner and outer, dream self and face self. Her dream self was her real self; the other was the one she turned to the world, moldable into whatever she needed it to be. Her dream self was who she *was*—who she would be, that is, if she ever made it out of this miserable hick hayseed worthless church-saturated town. The fact is, she was nineteen years old and had never been anywhere. She didn't have a car or money for a plane or a bus ticket, and she was too scared to hitchhike, which nobody hardly did anymore anyway because girl hitchhikers kept getting strangled and cut up, and she never could seem to meet somebody who was going somewhere important so she could cadge a ride. She would've taken a ride to anywhere that wasn't here, actually, even Texas, but where she really wanted to go was California. She'd been California dreaming since she first heard that song when she was ten. Back then, everybody went to California. Now, nobody did. Or nobody from her town anyway.

So sometimes she'd meet guys in bars on Monday night Sports Night or Thursday night Ladies Night, always hoping one of them was on his way someplace good so she could go with him. So far, no luck. The town had a church on practically every corner but only a few beer bars, plus the country-and-western nightclub inside the motel on the bypass, where she went sometimes when she could get somebody

17

to take her, but mostly she drank at one of the town bars: 3.2 beer on tap, which was pretty lousy, but if you kept at it, you could get a decent buzz. After a few beers, her face self would morph into her dream self, and she could make whoever she was talking to believe what she believed: that she was *somebody*—a mysterious, important person just passing through town. In the morning, her face self would rematerialize, and she'd get up, scrub it clean, and go to work.

Her main job was carhopping at A&W. It was the most miserable of her three jobs, but it paid the best, which was still crap. Her carhop self was cute and perky (C&P she called it—she'd read that in a movie magazine), flirty when it needed to be, and sometimes she'd be plunging out dimes and quarters from the metal change holder clipped to her belt and a workman in a pickup would say *keep the change, sugar,* or a church lady might say *that's all right, dear.* But it was never enough.

She also worked Wednesday afternoons at her mom's church because her mom's rheumatoid arthritis was so bad now she couldn't type up the Sunday bulletins anymore. Her mom had been the church secretary since forever and she still did the books because that wasn't as hard on her joints as typing, and the church paid her mom, and her mom paid her. She'd peck out the sermon titles and hymn numbers and prayer lists onto the stencil, run them off on the mimeograph machine in the office, and carry the stack of slick medicinal-smelling bulletins to the sanctuary to be handed out next Sunday. Then she'd go gliding between the pews straightening the hymnals and Holy Bibles and Visitor cards in the seatbacks and picking up the used Kleenexes left behind by the old ladies and the scribbled-on bulletins left behind by the little kids. Boring work, and completely nonlucrative, but it was for her mom, so she did it. Then she and her mom would sit through Wednesday night prayer meeting—the absolutely most boring of the three boring church services she went to with her mom every week—and afterwards they'd go home and watch *Little House on the Prairie* with their Swanson TV dinners on folding tables in the den.

Her third job was that she babysat. Always for the same couple, always on Friday nights. Six bucks a pop, which was supposed to work out to two dollars an hour but almost never did, because they almost never came home that early. They lived across town and went to her mom's church, but the man kept paperbacks in his nightstand that the preacher would have had a holy conniption cow if he ever saw. But she liked them, the books, or anyhow she read them, a little sick to her stomach sometimes, and excited, and scared. She'd wrestle the kids to bed—a boy and a girl, five and seven, who shrieked and fought like demons, but she'd bribe them with Pop-Tarts and not make them brush their teeth after, so generally she could get them asleep by nine—and then she'd go to the couple's bedroom and dig out whatever paperback was in the nightstand's bottom drawer.

She didn't know where he got them. Not the town library, for sure, though they always seemed a little thumbed-through and used-looking, with half-naked, red-lipsticked women on the covers, different hair colors but the same pouty lips and scared eyes, and sometimes a shadowy man standing over or behind them. There'd be a different book every week, buried under the same *TIME* magazine and yellow *National Geographic*. In the beginning she'd started reading at page one, until she realized she was never going to finish any of the stories because he changed them out so often, so she started skimming, looking for the good parts—one hand pressed to her panties, one ear cocked toward the driveway to hear when the couple came home.

But one night she missed.

The first Friday night in November. 1975. Cold and cloudy. Later, she'd try to trace back why it happened that night, but it didn't seem like there was any reason; she just didn't hear the station wagon pull up. The first thing she heard was the wife's voice, soft and puzzled, calling her name from the front room. Then the man's hard heels clicking along the hall. She slammed the book into the drawer, kicked the drawer shut, but he was already in the doorway, his eyes behind his glasses steady on her, his balding head backlit. He called over his shoulder, "She's back here checking on the kids, hon!"

She had on her Responsible Babysitter face now, very grown-up and efficient; she said she'd heard a noise and was making sure the windows were locked. Then the wife was behind him in the lighted hall, her ratted bouffant stiff as a rain bonnet, her eyes blurred with drink. The girl smiled her C&P smile, walked straight toward them, and they parted, let her through, followed her to the front room, the wife digging in her purse for the six dollars.

Outside, she got in the front seat for the man to run her home, like always, and, like always, she put on Committed Church Girl for the awkward ten-minute drive across town. She talked about her plans to be a missionary after she'd saved enough money to go to the local church-affiliated college. "Is that right," the man said. He was driving slower than usual, the smell of liquor wafting from him, very faint.

"'Go ye therefore,'" she said, her voice high and breathy, "'and teach all nations, baptizing them in the name of the Father and of the Son and of the Holy Ghost.' Of course, women can't baptize, but we can teach Bible lessons to the little children in Africa. We can win souls to Christ."

He turned left at the college, drove past the giant chapel where the students met daily for morning worship services, on toward the scattered dark buildings at the edge of campus, then on beyond that.

"Where are we going?" she said lightly. Not where are *you* going? Not where are you taking me? She'd given him *we* already. She'd already acquiesced. He turned onto an industrial side road, unpaved, drove a short distance, and parked beside a giant mound of gravel in an otherwise empty lot.

"Aren't we a little Nosey Parker," the man said, and switched off the engine.

"Beg pardon?"

"I didn't take you for a sneak." His voice was greasy, insinuating. "Maybe a lot of things I didn't take you for."

"I don't know what you're talking about." She put her hand on the door handle, peering past the gravel pile. Nothing out there. Only black prairie and the dim, distant lights along the bypass. She could see the neon slipper at the Cinderella Motel blinking—not the slipper itself, that garish pink outline, just the color flashing against the night clouds: pink, then gray again, then pink. "My mom's going to be worried," she said. "She might call your house."

"I don't think so."

"I think she might." But her voice sounded weak. Her mom was in bed hard asleep; she knew that. Pain meds and water glass on the nightstand. *The Tonight Show* murmuring on the portable TV. She whispered, "I'm not going to tell anyone."

"Tell them what?"

"Nothing." Maybe he didn't see her doing what she thought he saw? But then why would he drive her out here, call her a Nosey Parker and all that? The security light, buzzing on its tall pole, lit the car's interior in a faint lavender glow. "Anyhow," she chirped, her C&P voice, "I bet your wife will be worried if you don't get home soon."

"My wife's passed out on the couch."

"How do you know that?"

No answer. His eyes were unreadable behind his glasses. His left hand was on the steering wheel, his right hand buried in the shadow of his lap. She heard him unzip his trousers.

"Tell me," he said.

"What?"

"You know what." His hand was moving in his lap. "What you read."

"I wasn't reading, I was . . . looking for a Bible. You know, like how the Gideons put them in hotels? I just thought . . ." She gripped the door handle so tightly her fingers cramped. If he reached for her, she'd jump out. But he didn't reach for her. Only himself. "Tell me," he said again. His voice was guttural, not threatening, but it wasn't a request.

She stared hard across the field. Pink. Gray. Pink. Gray. A mile away at least. No road from here to there, just black bunchgrass and clumps of sumac. She turned to look behind, the way they'd come. The lights of the college twinkled small and white and inviting. That way was closer. But it also had roads. Which he could drive if he wanted to come after her.

"Describe it," the man whispered. "Tell me how it made you feel."

A cold hard fury swept through her, bursting upward from her gut, pouring out through her face, the top of her head. "God you're a creep," she said. Her voice was flat, emotionless. She jerked the door handle and got out. Reaching back into the floorboard for her purse, she said in her sultry *somebody* voice, "Preacher's going to be real interested in what you keep in your nightstand. So's your wife. So's my mom." The man's face was furious beneath the dome light. She could make out his eyes now, popping with rage. Also fear. "Your wee-wee's shriveling." She pointed. Then she slammed the door and started across the dark field.

She heard the car start. She kept going, stumbling over clumps of knotted grass, bumping into low shrubs, and, goddamn, it was cold. The car's engine growled behind her, but he didn't turn on the headlights, and he didn't drive away, so she kept walking. The night clouds were so low they reflected light from the town overhead, an eerie amber glow. Just enough to see by.

INSIDE the nightclub, liquor bottles were lined up in rows against the mirror behind the bar. She sat at the far end, away from the door, ordered a rum and Coke. All the money she had was what the wife gave her: six wrinkled bills crammed in her jeans pocket. The bartender barely glanced at her fake ID. "That'll be two dollars," he said. She gave him two. She was shivering. She glanced around. Friday night, after eleven, the place was crowded with older couples—like the age of the couple she babysat for—laughing and smoking cigarettes at the tiny tables, two-stepping around the tiny dance floor. She downed the rum and Coke, motioned for another, her Bored Sophisticate face. Four bucks down now.

In the mirror she checked out the single guys at the other end of the bar—two in cowboy hats, three in ball caps—trying to gauge which was most likely to buy her drinks and not expect her to go home with him. One of the cowboys met her gaze, a slight nod. She pulled up her Bedazzled Innocence face. But then a heavyset girl pushed in between them, took the empty stool next to her, cutting off her view. "I know you," the girl said, laughing.

"Really?" She eyed the girl. Long brown hair parted in the middle, round face, no makeup, no eyebrows. "I don't think so."

The girl laughed again, mouth open, shoulders shaking, but the laugh was silent, or inaudible anyway beneath the whine of Freddy Fender on the jukebox. She looked a bit like those old photos of Janis Joplin; otherwise, there was nothing familiar about her.

"What's your name?"

"You knew me as Sheila. I go by Snow now."

She'd never known anyone named Sheila. She didn't think. "Nice to meet you, Snow."

"Nice to see you again, Elaine."

Her throat jumped. She never told anyone that name. "I think you've got me confused with somebody else."

"Your name's Elaine, isn't it?"

Elaine turned to face the crowded room. "Not really," she said.

"Not really?"

"Nobody calls me that anymore." She caught the steady hot-pink glow of the giant neon slipper on the wall beside the Coors waterfall. "I go by Ella now."

Snow laughed again. This time it was audible, a yipped bark. "Ella," she said. "As in Cinder Ella. How original."

Elaine stood up to move to the other end of the bar.

"No. Stay." Snow touched her hand. "I'll quit teasing. Come on. Here, I'll buy you another rum and Coke." She had on Levi's, a man's work shirt, no jacket, no purse—and how did she even know what Elaine was drinking? But she pulled a twenty out of her shirt pocket and laid it on the bar. That was persuasive. Elaine sat. "Where do you know me from then?" she said.

"School."

"High school?"

"Saint Ig's."

"Saint *Ig's*?" This would be Saint Ignatius Catholic Girls School, which Elaine had been inside of exactly twice and surely did not ever attend. "You're crazy. We're Baptists."

Snow shrugged, swiped the bills left from the twenty off the bar and tucked them in her shirt. Elaine lifted the rum and Coke. "Thanks." She finished almost half. "Aren't you having one?"

"I don't drink," Snow said.

"What are you doing here then?"

"Looking for you."

"That," Elaine said, "is just weird."

Snow laughed her silent Buddha laugh. She waved the bartender over again, asked for a glass of water. Frowning, he blasted a stream from his mixer gun into a highball glass, plunked it ungraciously on the bar, lumbered back to the other end to pull draws for the cowboys. The music was suddenly very loud. Mickey Gilley wailing out "City Lights."

"A," Elaine called out over the music, "I don't know you, so how could you be looking for me? B, I didn't know myself I'd be here till half an hour ago, so how could you be looking for me *here*? And C . . . oh, forget it."

"When we were little," Snow yelled in her ear, "we used to play together in the school yard."

Elaine yelled in Snow's ear. "What school yard?"

"Saint Ig's!"

"Not possible!"

"There's lots that's not possible that happens anyway! Right?"

But Elaine's third drink was finished, and her mind was on the bartender and how soon he'd make his way back to this end and how much she had left of her babysitting money. Enough for one more drink—not nearly enough. She fluffed up her hair with both hands, Brunette Dolly Parton smiling at the cowboys.

"Like for instance!" Snow yelled in her ear, "I know about that creep in the station wagon!"

The music stopped just as Elaine's heart stopped. She stared at the weird girl beside her. "How?" she whispered. In the silence, Snow offered not her voiceless laugh but a slow Cheshire Cat smile. The opening licks of "Rhinestone Cowboy" swelled into the room, the world moved again, but Elaine didn't. She couldn't. She didn't have a face for this. She didn't have a voice.

"You don't need to worry about him," Snow said. "He's finished." The jukebox volume was lower now. "So, anyway, that's one job kaput. Right?"

Elaine didn't answer, but she knew, yes, it was. She couldn't bear to ever look at that creep's face again, imagine him fondling himself thinking of her reading his creepy porn, which also meant no more Sunday morning church, where he always sat on the fifth pew with his hellion kids and zombie wife rowed up beside him, which meant—

"You don't have to worry about that either," Snow said.

"What?"

"Your mom expecting you to go to church."

"Where are you coming up with this shit?"

"I'm telling you I know you."

"Well, I don't know *you*." Elaine tossed back the dregs of her drink, ice cubes clicking against her teeth; she motioned the bartender this way. He glanced up, nodded, turned away to pull another draw. She looked to the mirror, her frizzy dark halo peeking over the bottles. Jose Cuervo. Wild Turkey. Jack Daniel. Bacardi, her favorite. But she only drank well drinks—unless somebody else was buying. "Sorry," she mumbled.

"What do you want more than anything in the world?"

To get the hell out of this town.

"You want to leave this town."

Elaine's heart was pumping hard now. "You're creeping me out." She reached to the floor for her purse.

"So, what's stopping you," Snow said. Not a question. She held up three fingers, the last three—middle finger to pinkie, palm inward. "One, three jobs you hate, right?" She folded her pinkie into her palm. "Two, your mom." Ring finger, down. "Three, the fact you're actually a chicken shit." Middle finger still standing like a big fuck you.

"What'll it be?" The bartender had finally made it to this end.

"Rum and Coke." Elaine smiled, let her purse slide back to the floor. He was old, paunchy, grumpy. But he held the key.

"Make it Bacardi." Snow pulled a ten out of her shirt pocket.

The bartender used the jigger this time, measured carefully, erring on the stingy side. Snow slid a single back toward him when he brought the change. Good, Elaine thought. Maybe he'll be less nasty now. She picked up her drink.

"So: you only get three," Snow said. "But you got to say them out loud."

"Three what?" Elaine said. "Drinks?" But suddenly she knew. "Like, wishes?"

"You could call them that. Or dreams."

"Dreams."

"Tell me what you want. Say it out loud."

"I want to get the hell out of this town."

Snow nodded, smiling encouragement.

"I want to *be* somebody."

Snow nodded again. Waited. It took a long time for Elaine to say the third. It was almost a whisper:

"I want my mom to be okay."

Snow smiled. "Done."

A cold strand of barbed wire tightened across Elaine's chest.

"No," Snow said, "nothing like that. I mean *okay* okay. Look," she nodded over her shoulder toward the male drinkers down the bar, "they're not who you want to be dealing with tonight. Am I right?"

She was right. But Elaine was in no mood to say so.

"So let's get out of here," Snow said. "We'll go take a look at your mom, you can see for yourself, then we'll head out to the highway."

"You're crazy."

"Not crazy at all." The silent open-mouthed laugh, the crinkled blue eyes. Snow swung herself off the barstool, picked up Elaine's purse, and started toward the door. A bearlike side-to-side shuffle. She was built square, like a man. Elaine had a few seconds to decide. Scream out over the jukebox *Stop her, that bitch stole my purse!* And deal with the cowboys' attention, the middle-aged couples turning to stare, the stingy bartender maybe calling the cops—or follow her. Elaine finished her Bacardi and Coke, slid off the stool, and followed.

In the parking lot, Snow sat behind the wheel of a tan, beat-up Volkswagen Beetle. "Give us a push," she said through the open door.

"Seriously?" Elaine said.

"Seriously. Starter's out. Look, we're on an incline." And indeed they were. Elaine went behind the car and pushed, grunting, until the car started to roll down the slope; when it got up to speed, she heard Snow pop the clutch, and the engine rattled to life, a thousand pebbles in a giant tin can. For a split second, Elaine could have kicked herself, figuring that's the last she'd see of her purse, which contained no money but did hold her favorite hairbrush, her strawberry lip gloss, an unopened pack of Dentyne, and her very valuable fake ID. But the VW slowed, and Snow reached over to push open the passenger door. Elaine trotted to catch up. The engine sounded louder inside than out. Snow tossed her purse into her lap, and Elaine wrapped her arms around it like a pet. Everything was so weird now, she wasn't surprised when Snow turned at all the right streets, drove directly to Elaine's mother's house. The Beetle rolled to a stop out front. Snow didn't downshift or push in the clutch, so the engine died. Elaine could see a light on in the kitchen—the stove light, the way her mom always left it—but otherwise the front of the house was dark. She dug out her house key. "Thanks for the ride," she said. But Snow was already outside the car.

In the lightless living room, she heard laughter burbling from the television in her mother's bedroom. Snow stood close beside her. She was shorter than Elaine. She smelled like patchouli. She walked like a burr stuck to Elaine's side along the dark hall. The bedside light was on in her mom's room, the frilly blue shade giving a soft wash to the stale air. Ed McMahon was chuckling on the television. The audience tittered. Her mother was asleep on her side, legs pulled up, hands folded beneath her cheek like a prayer. Elaine could see her shoulders rising and falling in slow, even breaths. She looked beautiful. Peaceful. Calm. Gentle.

"See?" Snow whispered.

"I wish she could be like this all the time," Elaine murmured.

"She can," Snow said. "She is."

The TV switched to a commercial. Snow tugged Elaine's sleeve. "We'd better go."

"What? I'm home. You go."

"It's almost midnight."

"So?"

Snow tipped back her head to gaze at her. No silent laugh. No smile. Her face was quietly serious. "If you don't go now, Ellie," she said, "you're never going."

"Bullshit," Elaine said, her voice low. She didn't want to wake her mom. "And what's with 'Ellie'? Don't call me that."

"Who are you then?"

Who was she? C&P. Church Girl. Responsible Babysitter. Bored Sophisticate. Nosey Parker. *Somebody*. "I don't know," she said. She remembered now. She thought she remembered. An unfamiliar school yard, a tetherball pole, the trampled dirt circle. Leaning back against the hard metal pole, her knees dirty; her mom would be so mad. Behind her, on the other side of the pole, a girl who was almost her friend. Telling secrets.

"You good with Elaine, then?"

Elaine shook her head. Then she nodded. The rum was wearing off. Her mouth was dry. She had a bad headache. The *Tonight Show* music came on.

"Where do you want to go?" Snow said.

"California."

"It's a big state."

"I know. L.A. maybe."

"L.A.'s good."

"Are you going?"

"Of course."

"I can't leave my mom."

"Okay." Snow shrugged, walked out of the room. Why didn't she just let her go? Later, she would ask herself this, too, and find no more sensible reason for it than for why she hadn't heard the creep's station wagon pull into their carport. The clock in the front hall began chiming the hour. She moved quietly to the bed, kissed two fingers, placed them gently on her mother's warm cheek. "Bye, Mama," she whispered.

Outside, Snow stood in the empty street where the Beetle had been. She had on a denim jacket now, a red scarf tied around her forehead like a headband, an army duffel bag on the cement at her feet. She handed Elaine her purse. "I told you it was getting late. We'll have to walk it from here." She bent down, picked up a buzzing June bug stranded on its back beneath the streetlight, set it upright on the curb. "Come," she said, and began walking back along the street toward the highway.

Tahlequah Triptych

1973–1978

The Color of Verdigris

Hungry

That Grief, That Fury

The Color of Verdigris

The room smells of peroxide and mold and the thinnest tang of old urine. The girl stands in the center, a white towel draped over her shoulders. Her hands are open at her sides, empty. She watches her eyes, two halos the color of verdigris, staring into the mirror over the sink. The faucet drips. In the unit next door, a laugh-track rattles. She waits.

She thought once of bringing a gun to this room. Her father's .22 would not be soon missed from its place in the receipt box beneath the counter in the motel office. Not missed soon enough. But that had been her last birthday, when her mother called from Denver in the early hours of the morning promising money and a present in the mail—next week, just as quick as her check came, the week after, no later, and maybe Colorado next summer—and Reva forgot the pistol in the receipt box and waited for the present, the money, the trip to Denver that never materialized. Tomorrow she will turn seventeen.

She has visions of herself. Tomorrow she will walk into the school and be no longer invisible. Her nose will be shapely; her ruddy, pocked cheeks will be smooth. Tonight, when she's finished, she'll walk across the parking lot, around the gaping sky-blue square of the swimming pool, drained for the winter, the metal chairs stacked against the cyclone fence, and she'll enter the office. Her father will be there. She will stare at him, there, where he sits with his feet propped behind the counter, a Camel burning between two fingers, his newspaper loose in his hands. When his face opens, then darkens, she'll tell him: *It's my life, Father.* She will call him Father. *I didn't have to ask you. I don't need your permission for nothing. I left you a long time ago, old man.* She might say that. *I left you years ago—you didn't see it?*

And she had. Left him when she was thirteen and they'd moved to the town (his town, not hers, not her mother's); when he'd left the army, left her mother, moved back to Oklahoma and bought this tatty motel and painted it green. She'd walked from the apartment in back of the office to the streets of the town, to the junior high school, and found she was invisible. Found her thin arms and long legs had grown bony and useless, her face sharp, red bumps on her forehead and cheekbones, how very easy it was to hang her curtain of hair in front of her face and vanish. She'd left her father when she discovered that she herself had disappeared.

But tomorrow will be different. Tomorrow she'll walk through the halls with her hair back, her face changed. Beautiful. She sees it. She can see it. She dreams.

Next door someone flicks through the channels, the sound rising and changing and falling. Reva watches the mirror. The verdigris eyes stare back at her. She believes they are beautiful in their short fringe of black lashes: the color of rivers, of new sage, of sea water. She believes they are the only thing beautiful in her face. The brows above are thick, nearly nestled together, like two woolly bears crawling to meet. The nose between is hawk-billed and ugly, but she will not look. It isn't hard not to. The mirror is fogged—not from steam but from age and paltriness, the foil backing peeled away in odd places—and the girl stands just so, where her eyes meet her eyes, and she dreams.

It begins. She raises her gaze and in the mirror she sees it: her lank hair parted in the middle, hanging to her shoulders, dripping chemicals onto the skimpy white towel, from dun brown to orange yellow, lightening: the change. She holds her breath. Music swells from next door, then the bland chirp of a commercial, and she drifts back from it, waiting for the last possible moment, hoping to recognize, and stop the process, at the precise penultimate moment between white blonde and destruction.

In the motel office, her father looks at her. He says nothing. His face does not open. He does not even blink. In silence she pushes past him, replaces the key on the pegboard, strolls back to her room.

At school the next day, two boys follow her from her locker to algebra, whispering sexy, dirty things. Her history teacher looks at her, glances away, turns quickly to look again. Her gym teacher calls her, for the first time, by name. In the restroom she gazes up into the high tilted mirror over the sink and sees her face thinner, duskier, her eyes brighter. Her hair shines in the light from the window—the broken ends ragged, glinting like dimes. Behind her, two girls whisper together, laughing. As she turns to push through the door, away from their whispers and giggles, she hears one of them say it, a little croak, like a tree frog, meant for the girl's ears: "Gaw, she looks like a skag!"

Visible. Reva smiles to herself as she steps out into the green-tiled hall.

She leaves her father's motel the day after graduation, but she does not leave the town. She moves into a white rundown house near campus with three longhairs she met at the QuikTrip. Her roommates are cool. They smoke dope and drink beer, and they don't try to sleep with her. They all came to the college from somewhere else. Reva tells them she's an orphan, that she grew up in California. She moved to the town to live with her uncle, she says, a fat redheaded drunk who once tried to rape her. But she stabbed him in his fat freckled belly with a steak knife, and he kicked her out. This is why she never has any money.

Sometimes she sees her father in town driving along the main street or sitting in his Pontiac by the teller's window at the drive-in bank. She turns and goes the other direction when she sees him. Once, coming out of Safeway with one of her roommates, she heard his voice calling her from across the parking lot. She shoved her grocery sack at the roommate and walked quickly toward the alley, stood next to the stinking dumpster behind the store for half an hour. When she came back to the parking lot, her father's car was gone, but so was her roommate's, and she had to walk home. Now she scans every lot for a green Pontiac before she steps outside.

She gets a job at the pizza parlor near campus, cash under the table plus tips; she walks home at night stinking of tomato sauce and pepperoni, brings her roommates free pizzas when she can. In January, for her birthday, the roommates give her a party. They wrap a baggie of Panama Red in tinfoil, tape a packet of rolling papers to the front, and put it on the kitchen table beside three six-packs of Coors tied together with string, because, as they tell her, jumping into the room, whooping and laughing: three times six equals eighteen.

Deep in the night, while the party swirls in the kitchen and spills out drunkenly into the cold yard, Reva goes into the bathroom. She looks at her face in the mirror. The light from the bare bulb is above and behind her, and she cannot see the small, pitted scars on her cheeks or the threads of broken vessels in her eyes. She sees only the sea green color and her white hair backlit like a halo. She's drunk, a little stoned, and she thinks she is beautiful.

But summer comes, and two of the roommates move home with their parents. The third says she can stay if she pays half the rent. Reva lands a job as an understudy dancer at the outdoor drama on the edge of the town. She lies her way into the audition, says she studied ballet, jazz, and tap in Colorado. The choreographer asks her to move across the floor with the others—they're rehearsing in the gym at the Sequoyah boarding school outside town, basketball hoops and a shiny wooden stage at one end—and Reva is a little high, and the music is drum-filled and pounding, and she goes with it, floating. The choreographer begins making cuts. She goes to him where he stands near the stage apron and tells him quietly that she's part Cherokee. He looks at her, doubtful, and she pulls her bleached hair back in a hand-gripped ponytail, turns her face to catch the light. When the final cuts are made and all but eighteen auditioners are thanked and dismissed, Reva remains. She's not going to be a full dancer but an understudy who'll go on if one of the female dancers gets sick. The rest of the nights she'll be a villager shuffling along the Trail of Tears with the extras. It is enough.

The choreographer stages the show in five days and flies back to New York, leaving the dance captain to rehearse the troupe until opening. The dance captain is tall and blond and lithe and beautiful. His name is Eugene. For a week Reva and the other understudies just watch. Then, the day before the big move to the amphitheater for dress rehearsals, Eugene calls out to four dancers to take a break and puts the four understudies in—two males and two females. He stands at the lip of the stage, clapping, calling out: *five, six, seven, eight! and step, and step, and kick ball change, and left, right, left, kick! and kick, and step, and turn, turn, turn, kick!*

She tries. She watches the dancers in front of her, but she can't translate what she sees into her own body. The turns make her dizzy, she doesn't know how to spot, or rather, she knows—train your gaze on one spot on the far wall, keep it there, turn your body, then whip your head fast and come back with your eyes on the same spot—but she comes out of the spins gyrating across the floor, arms flailing, facing the wrong direction. She can't remember the combinations,

has to stop and watch the others, try to transcribe what they're doing into her own arms and legs. She's always a half step behind. The
other female understudy, a chubby brunette with calves like baseballs
and eyes like wet mud, moves easily beside her, picking up every turn.

She doesn't fit. She never fits. If only there were mirrors. If only
she could see herself as she dreams—head lifted, neck elongated,
arms stretched to her gracefully cupped fingers, thighs firm, feet certain, her beautiful eyes brilliant in the sunlight as she turns—then
she could learn it. But the gym is not a dance studio: there are no
mirrors lining the walls, only the clutter of dance bags and pop cans,
the high louvered windows overhead, the smell of sweat and floor
wax; there is nothing to reflect the girl back to herself. She stumbles,
almost falls, stands motionless as the others whirl past.

Eugene leaps off the stage, calling to the others to *keep moving!*
Keep moving! And he comes and dances the combination in front of
her, saying, *feet first, find your feet*, and when Reva is moving again,
he comes behind her, circles her wrists with his fingers and guides
her arms like a puppet, pressing his body against her back. She can
feel him, she can smell him, salt and damp sheets, and it is now, in
this moment, in the hot early morning of the twelfth day of rehearsal,
that she falls in love.

At noon, when Eugene turns off the tape recorder and the dancers clap languidly and groan and move toward their cigarettes and
dance bags, Reva stands at the back of the gym, hating them. She
hates their slanting necks, their leotards and liniments, their slouch-
ing fatigue. She hates the careless way they joke as they file out the
door, Eugene tall and pale in the midst of them; how they all know
him, know each other, know *something* she has never known and
never will. She shakes her head no when the understudy with mud
eyes turns to ask if she wants a ride. Reva remains in the gym, alone,

practicing in the stink of mildew and floor wax and the wet clinging heat. Going over the combinations, trying to learn them kinesthetically. Trying to force the movements, like memory, inside her limbs.

THE show opens, and she loses her pizza job because she can't work her evening shifts anymore. Her roommate, who drove her to the gym for rehearsals, works nights and can't give her rides now. She wants to ask Eugene if she can ride to the amphitheater with him, but she's afraid, so she asks the understudy with mud eyes instead. She promises gas money as soon as they get paid. In the women's dressing room, Reva stands at the mirror and watches the dancers painting their skins in long, bored strokes with damp sponges dipped in jars of loose powder labeled Texas Dirt. She reaches for her own sponge. She looks at herself while she applies her makeup—deep fuchsia for her lips, black eyeliner, dark green on her eyelids—but after she's put on her wig, she turns away. She does not like looking at her pocked, painted skin beneath the bulky black braids. She leaves the dressing room and sits outside on the walkway.

With her eyes, she follows Eugene as he paces in the wings, bending and stretching, twisting his body into impossible contortions, breathing deep. His painted skin is rust red, his blond hair dyed black. Still, she loves him. Every night she puts herself to sleep feeling his body behind her, his warm, comforting presence. Peaceful. Protective. Like an angel. Eugene doesn't feel her watching him, or if he does, he doesn't show it. He never looks back.

It is scarcely dusk when the play begins. The stage lights come up, the music starts, dirgelike and mournful, and Reva joins the others making their lugubrious trek across the stage. The wind howls over the loudspeakers. The sad music soars. She practiced this part during dress rehearsals, though there is nothing to practice, really. They just walk. The principal actors, the dancers, the villagers, all wrapped in ragged blankets, emerge from stage right, coughing, stumbling across to stage left. Some of them fake helping the old ones and the fallen; others pretend to die and get carried offstage by their fellows. As soon as they exit, they race around backstage to the first entrance to begin the slow tortured journey again. In this way, it appears there are many, many more Cherokees on the Trail of Tears than are actually getting paid.

All the while, over the loudspeaker, a woman's voice is telling the story of how the Cherokee people were forced from their homelands in the east to this new land in Indian Territory, how they were cheated of food, shelter, how a quarter of the people died on the march. But Reva is not interested in this part of her job. She wants to be one of the dancers. Beneath their ragged blankets, the dancers wear fringed buckskin dresses and leggings, their costumes for the first dance. Beneath her ragged blanket, Reva wears a villager's coarse brown shift.

And so it is. Throughout the play, she stands off to the side, an extra, a female body filling up space on the stage. She changes costumes as the pageant sweeps through the years—a Southern Belle ball gown as a student at the Cherokee Female Seminary, a green pinafore as a townsperson in the Statehood Day dance—but she never takes center stage. From the side she watches the female dancers, moving with them invisibly, inside herself, her fingers counting the steps against her palm. She watches Eugene, his long body a perfection as he dances the lead in the Green Corn Dance, the Ribbon Dance, the climactic Phoenix Dance near pageant's end. Sometimes, while it is still dusk and there's enough light to see, Reva looks up at the audience, though she's been told not to do this. But she likes to see them, these hundreds of middle-aged tourists, and sometimes their

children, seated in rows upon rows up the steep steps, fanning them-
selves with their programs, their eyes riveted to the stage. *Me*, her
mind whispers. *Look at me.*

Every night, as the players leave the dressing rooms and meander
toward their cars, she listens to their chatter to hear which bar Eugene
is going to, whose apartment for a party. She bums a ride and follows
him there, hangs near his table or leans against the counter in the
kitchen—laughing in the wrong places, drinking beer, talking too
loud. On Sundays, their day off, she walks to the apartment complex
where he stays with three other dancers and lies on a towel beside
the swimming pool, her skin darkening in the June sun.

The third week of performance, Reva dyes her hair black. That evening she goes onstage in her own hair, as the Cherokee villagers do,
and nobody says anything. For a week she gets away with it. But one
night the show's owner, known as the Colonel for his military-style
strictness and also because he was once a colonel in the U.S. Army,
watches the show from the top of the amphitheater. He speaks to the
stage manager, who catches Reva as she's leaving the dressing room.
The stage manager tells her the cheap dye job shows up brassy under
the stage lights, and her hair is too thin and stringy to be real Indian
hair anyway. She has to wear the wig. A rebellion rises in her. She
wants to snap at him as she would snap at her father: *I don't have to
do anything you say, old man.* But she doesn't snap. To do that could
get her fired. And then she would lose Eugene.

She dreams. Awake dreams and sleeping dreams. In the awake
dreams, Eugene turns to look at her, and sees her, really *sees* her, for
the first time: her sculpted cheekbones and arched brows, her somber eyes the color of verdigris. A soft rain is falling. He takes her
hand, leads her into the dance. In her daydreams, she is pale blonde
again, and beautiful, though in reality she's afraid to rebleach her
hair. It's already so damaged and broken. She'll wait till the end

of summer. Or at least until . . . well, sometime, she thinks. In her sleeping dreams, Eugene is also blond again, a brilliance, a shining light. But mostly, in her sleeping dreams, it is the feel of him behind her, the protective warmth, the cherishing feeling, wrapped around her being like a glove.

THEN it is midsummer, the air hot and thick with water so that their painted skins run in red rivulets as they wait in the wings in the late humid dusk. The choreographer has flown in from New York to see the show, to see his dancers, his choreography, the continuing work of his protégé Eugene. The dancers are nervous, high-pitched and coltish, the boys darting from the dressing room half naked in their dance belts, chittering *Maar-tin, Maar-tin.* They all hope to join his New York dance company one day. Gone is their feigned boredom, the languid ennui they've worn these past weeks like the Texas Dirt on their bodies. Reva listens to their excited talk with disdain. An afterparty at the lake is nothing special. They party every night, don't they? By the lake, in the bars, on the riverbank, at somebody's apartment. Now they're acting like the king of the world is here.

Still, she rides to the lake party with the understudy with mud eyes. They've formed a silent contract over the summer: both outsiders, both invisible to the rest of the dancers, they travel together. Reva has good contacts for dope; the understudy with mud eyes has a car. After they arrive at the party—any party, every party—they do not acknowledge each other.

A jumble of granite boulders lines the lake shore, obsidian in the starlight, in the blue-black night of the new moon. The lake stretches black into blackness, a few hazy lights winking on the far shore answering the starlight: four tiny human orbs blinking back at the sky. At the water's edge a large, flat rock, the width of a small stage, juts over the lake's surface. It is here the dancers crowd with their coolers of beer and their smokes and their tequila. Two boys, shrieking laughter into the darkness, build a fire in the barbecue pit nearest the boulders. The dancers laugh and drink in the firelight, leap from the flat rock into the black water—their splashes, their singing like the endless sound of celebration.

Reva does not go into the water. She is afraid of the still depths, of what cannot be seen in the dark beneath the unbroken surface. She sits on the rim of rock farthest from the water, her arms folded around her legs, her feet tucked up near her body. She's aware of Eugene sitting in a lawn chair just outside the rim of firelight, and next to him, on the periphery, but dominant with his New York accent and dry wit, the choreographer holding court. There's so much drinking and laughter and splashing. Reva takes the Cuervo bottle when it is passed, listens to their jokes and their laughter. Listens, and does not talk.

When gray light begins to meld with the blackness and the stars begin disappearing, Reva stands and stretches. The beer is gone. The tequila is gone. The two dancers who drove to town on a beer run an hour ago have not come back. She looks out over the water, can make out the dim outline of the hills on the far side. The four winking lights have disappeared. She turns and weaves past the dying fire, looking for Mud Eyes to get a ride home.

In the light space between trees, on top of a picnic table, she sees them sitting close together, the outsides of their thighs touching. The choreographer's balding forehead shows white in the grayness; his arm is intimate, casual, around Eugene's neck. Their voices are a low murmur, a supplication, an explanation, a benediction. Eugene lifts his face, and the choreographer, with great tenderness, kisses him on the lips. Comprehension passes over her, lapping like the waves of her drunkenness. She knew this, of course. Why didn't she know this? She watches them, fascinated, contemptuous. Excited. When they lie back and the sounds of their breaths, the sight of their hands moving pulls a warm, unwilled arousal from her, she turns and walks back toward the water. She finds Mud Eyes making out with a young Cherokee boy, a villager from the drama who sometimes follows the dancers to parties. Promising them dope from her roommate's stash, she tells them the party is over, no more booze is coming tonight, they might as well drive back to town.

They arrive at the rented house in the yellow surprise of early daylight. The living room smells of ashtrays and smoke and stale beer. Reva puts a tape in the tape deck and turns it low and gives Mud Eyes a quaalude. She touches the boy's palm when she hands him the joint, looks into his eyes, and together they wait on the broken couch for the understudy with mud eyes to pass out.

Late in the afternoon, when her roommate wanders bed-headed into the kitchen to roll joints and make coffee, Reva stares up at him from beneath a ratty crocheted afghan on the living room floor. Beside her, the young boy snores softly, curled toward her, one arm thrown over her chest. Mud Eyes is asleep on the couch. Reva knows what the roommate thinks. She doesn't care. She doesn't try to explain anything. She gets up from the floor, goes to pee, then to her room, where she shuts the door, crawls onto the bed. She is sick with a hangover, nauseous with fear. Broken with loss.

DETACHMENT settles in. She no longer laughs in the wrong places or follows Eugene. She still goes to the parties, but she's stopped riding with Mud Eyes. She avoids her backstage, cadges rides with other dancers to work. For a few nights, at the theater, the Cherokee boy tries to talk to her. He asks her how she's doing, follows her with his eyes. She ignores him. He's only in high school. He does not own a car. Very soon he ignores her, too. Completely. If they're in the same cramped backstage area waiting to walk on for the Trail, he acts as if he doesn't see her. If his gaze happens to accidentally pass over her, there's no flicker of recognition. She's relieved, and furious. She didn't sleep with him. Or, well, yes, she slept with him, but only slept. He tried, but she kept pushing his hands away. They wrestled on the floor till he quit finally and fell asleep. Now he acts like he got what he wanted and then dropped her. But she didn't give it to him. She's never screwed anybody, as a matter of fact. Though that's a truth she wouldn't want people to know.

Reva's stories grow wilder, their telling more frequent. In the dressing room, she paints her skin, applies her eye makeup, rattling along about her plans to move back to California when summer's over. She went to high school in Palo Alto, you know, with Joan Baez and Grace Slick. Her boyfriend was a roadie for Led Zeppelin on their first American tour, but now he's a drummer with Leon Russell. She hardly ever sees him. She's going to move out to L.A. to live with him next fall. She's being treated for cancer, did you know? Also epilepsy. She has to go to Tulsa for the treatments. But she's much better now. When her great-aunt dies in England, she'll come into a huge inheritance. She might move to London. Or probably Paris. When she lived in Colorado she trained for the Olympics. The lies fall from her lips like rubies, like ashes. They fall to the earth like broken teeth. No one bothers to tell her the lies don't make any sense.

In town, she neglects to watch for her father's Pontiac. He surprises her once, pulling up beside her where she's sitting in her roommate's car at Sonic. Her father stands at the passenger-side window yelling at her to roll down the glass. Reva sits staring straight ahead.

"Man," her roommate says, "your dad's freaking weird."

"Let's go," she says.

"We didn't get our food yet."

"So? We didn't pay for it either. Let's go to Burger Chef. I'll buy."

Her father is still standing beside the kiosk yelling when they pull out of the slot.

ONE of the female dancers develops shin splints and has to sit out for two weeks. It's almost the end of the season, but Eugene calls everyone in for rehearsal. The concrete stage is miserable at midday, the air stifling from an overnight rain. There are small puddles in low spots around the stage, evaporating quickly as the dancers do their stretches and gripe and moan. "Music to my ears, lovelies," Eugene says, quoting Martin. He rehearses both understudies, but Reva stopped practicing with her fingers weeks ago. She can't remember the steps, their proper order. She doesn't really try. Eugene tells Mud Eyes she'll take the injured dancer's place tonight. Reva tells herself she doesn't care. And she doesn't, really. Not until Eugene pulls her aside as the others are strolling toward their cars in the sweltering afternoon.

"What's the matter with you?" His grip is tight on her arm.

"What?" she says. "Nothing."

"We've cut you so much slack. If I didn't need two understudies, you'd be gone now."

"I can go, no problem."

"I don't want you to go. I want you to quit calling in sick, quit half-assed doing your job when you're here. I want you to quit coming to the theater drunk."

"I don't come drunk."

"You come reeking. Listen. Reva. Go get your head straight. Practice the effing combinations. Come in this evening ready to work. I'll see about putting you in next week."

That night, for the first time in weeks, she watches the dancers. Specifically, she watches Mud Eyes. A kind of rage seethes in her, a sorrow, a yearning. It has nothing to do with Mud Eyes, or not her specifically. Only that she has taken Reva's rightful place. *I can do that. I can do it.* Her teeth grind in her jaw in time with the music. Her fingers dance against her palms. It is Saturday night, and the amphitheater is packed—a thousand white tourists with popcorn and cardboard fans watching the tragedy of the Cherokees. In the Civil War scenes, cannons boom over the loudspeakers, just as they boom every night. Flash pots explode on the mountain, like always, but this night something explodes inside Reva when she hears the audience gasp. The players are running every direction, and Reva runs with them. Unscripted, melodramatically, she screams out that she's been shot, falls down center stage. Two actors have to lift her and carry her off so the pageant can continue.

In the dressing room, she changes for the Statehood Day dance with her heart pounding, her face flushed, her eyes glistening beautifully in the mirror. The other dancers say nothing to her—they're rushing through their costume changes. The music starts, a tinkly ragtime beat, and Reva walks out onto the side stage, where she's supposed to stand among the townspeople in her green pinafore, swaying and clapping for the dancers doing their syncopated ragtime center stage. But Reva jumps up onto the stage-right revolve and begins dancing the Statehood Day dance full out, kicking her legs high, sashaying her skirts like a can-can dancer: whooping, shouting, creating the steps as she dances.

At the end of the night, the stage manager stands frowning in the dressing room doorway. The other dancers are quiet, smearing cold cream on their faces, tissuing it off. He tells Reva to put all her costumes in the hamper, take her personal items with her. She can pick up her check on Monday.

"But why?"

"Last chance is last chance. Or didn't you know that?"

It is Mud Eyes who sees her standing alone in the dark parking lot and offers her a ride back to town. Mud Eyes who tells her the Colonel had guests watching the show from the VIP seats that evening—the state's lieutenant governor, the Cherokee principal chief, their wives and cronies. "Tough luck," she says as she pulls up in front of Reva's shitty rented house. "Sucky timing. Who knew?" Her voice oozes sympathy. Reva doesn't believe an ounce of it. Mud Eyes asks if she wants a ride to the river tomorrow.

"What for?" Reva asks. Then she remembers the end-of-season company picnic and float trip scheduled for their day off. Mud Eyes shrugs, shifts into reverse, turns to look behind her. "No, wait," Reva says. "I mean, yeah. Sure. What time?"

SHE dresses for the picnic in front of the bathroom mirror. Halter top and cutoffs. Waterproof mascara. She's plucked her brows so ruthlessly they've almost disappeared. She draws herself new ones. Last night's rain left the air muggy again—she heard the crashes of thunder in her dreams—but brilliant sunlight slashes now through the window next to the sink. The pancake makeup on her forehead and pitted cheeks is too orange. Her hair is dull, flat black, almost greenish, the split ends ragged. She has no scissors. No bleach. She pulls her hair tight into a bun at the top of her head, holds it there with her fist as the sorrow and rage pour through. Her eyes are wide-eyed scared; she heaves, swallows deep, furious, sick with self-loathing. A car horn honks in front of the house. Reva releases her grip, scrapes her hair down in front of her face with her fingers.

At the river she hangs back by the car while Mud Eyes stumbles down the slope lugging her ice chest. Below, on the flat stony expanse of the gravel bar, the others are goofing with laughter as they place their beer coolers and food sacks, their bulgy blue-and-white bags of charcoal, their giant inflated innertubes. One guy is tightening the straps holding a metal canoe on the back of his truck. The others will rent from one of the canoe businesses lining the river, Reva thinks, or else use one of those innertubes. Float trips are a big tourist draw in the town, as big as the outdoor drama, but Reva has never floated the river herself. She's never had the money, or a partner to paddle with, or the chance. Like so much else in my life, she thinks in a wash of self-pity. She looks around for the Cherokee boy, but he isn't here. None of the villagers are here—only the white actors and dancers, the cool guys from the stage crew, the stage manager, one of the ladies from the costume shop. Eugene is here, of course, holding court from the tailgate of somebody's pickup. The other dancers are ringed around him—some standing, some sitting on the stony ground, looking up at him, laughing. What's he saying?

Reva stands smoking a cigarette in the parking area with the car door open. Why did she come? Mud Eyes only brought her to rub her face in it, right? Her total humiliation, the fact Eugene chose Mud Eyes to fill in for the dance, the fact Reva got sacked. She watches the other understudy plunk down her ice chest next to the tailgate, fold her chunky legs beneath her and settle to the ground in the half circle of dancers. Oh, but she's not an understudy now, is she? She's one of them. Mud Eyes takes the joint a male dancer hands her. Go ahead, Reva thinks, spurt out your smoke, cough and laugh, pass the joint to the next dancer, lean back on your pudgy, stiff little arms. You're one of them now. Reva slams the car door closed, tosses her smoke, starts down the bank in her flip-flops. She heads to the nearest cooler, digs out a can of Coors, and strides to the water's edge.

The river is high for mid-August, swollen with the recent rains, a muted, murky green. Small branches and bits of debris dance along, swirling in the current. Reva drains her beer, crushes the can in the middle, and throws it into the water. The bobbing gold-colored can disappears downstream. She feels their eyes on her. They're whispering behind their hands, *she's not a member anymore, she's not one of us, what's she's doing here?* But when the girl turns to make her way back to the cooler, no one is looking at her. They're throwing frisbees, pouring lighter fluid on charcoal, gathering wood for the fire. Somebody brought a portable tape deck; it's playing Fleetwood Mac. One of the dancers is standing on top of a picnic table swaying and waving her arms.

The Styrofoam lid squeaks when Reva lifts it from the ice chest. She digs out three beers, tucks one under her arm, sets the lid down crooked, heads back to the river. Why do they call this a gravel bar? she wonders as she sits. It's not gravel, not like the sharp little rocks on a gravel road. The river stones are small, smooth, pale, oval, rounded by the caressing, tumbling water for years. Even smooth stones aren't comfortable beneath her butt and legs, though. Reva stands up, goes and drags one of the giant innertubes to the water's edge. She sits in it, her butt in the open center, arms and legs draped over the hot tar-smelling sides. Must be for a freaking tractor, she thinks. Or one humongous truck. She chugs her beers, tosses the cans toward the water as she finishes, gets to her feet and sways toward the cooler. Or maybe it's a different cooler, who knows? Who cares?

Within an hour, she is very drunk. She feels herself drifting, dreaming in half sleep. The angel of light is behind her, his warmth, his beautiful comfort. After a while she surrenders; she falls asleep face up, cradled in the innertube's black embrace, one arm over her eyes. She doesn't know when the hot dogs are served, isn't aware when the two vans arrive in the parking area pulling trailers stacked with canoes, and the players climb in, hooting and shouting, to be driven upriver so they can float back down here to the gravel bar. It's only when she comes awake later, with her mouth dry, her thighs and belly burning, her head pounding, that she notices the quiet. She looks around for Eugene, but he's not here. Mud Eyes is not here. The stage manager's not here. No one's here except the costume shop lady and three of the older actors, sitting in the shade of an oak tree up the bank a ways. Reva blinks. Her mouth is so dry. She wants a beer. Or something. She wants something. A person should never drink beer on a sweltering hot summer afternoon. It just makes you thirstier.

She climbs awkwardly out of the innertube and goes to one of the coolers, but there are only a few cans of store-brand pop floating in the melting ice. She goes to another ice chest, then another, but they're all emptied of beer. She thinks the three actors and the costume shop lady are watching her. Are they watching her? She doesn't look up. She digs a Shasta cola out of a cooler and downs it in a few gulps, then goes to the innertube and drags it into the shade of a river willow, and sits. The rubber is burning hot from the sun, but she doesn't care. So is she. She doesn't need a mirror to tell her. She can feel her skin stretched tight, her forehead and cheeks screaming red under her makeup. But when the sunburn turns to tan, she thinks, my eyes will be greener. She knows this. She's seen it before. The river water is green too now, rain-swollen and murky, but it is not a beautiful bluish green. Like her eyes. The color of verdigris. God, she's so hot. And so thirsty. They took all the damn beer. She gets up and drags the innertube toward the water. If she paddles with her hands and feet, she thinks, as fast as the river is running, she might catch up with the others. She might catch up with Eugene.

By the time the floaters begin to arrive at the gravel bar, paddling leisurely downstream, slapping the water with their paddles, shouting as they jump into the shallow water and drag their canoes, scraping, onto the stones, everyone has forgotten the girl. No one notices she's missing—not the costume shop lady or the three actors, not the dance captain or the stage manager or the other dancers, not even the female understudy, Melinda, until she's ready to go home.

She begins to ask if anyone has seen Reva. They haven't. They don't remember. She was here a minute ago. Wasn't she just here?

Two days later, when the sheriff comes to the amphitheater to ask questions, the players are not sure. She was found in a logjam seven miles downriver, the sheriff tells them, almost all the way to Tenkiller Lake. A deflated innertube was wrapped around her middle. Her face and limbs were scratched by debris. Her family has been notified. Her father says she worked here. No foul play is suspected, he reassures them. Coroner's report says clearly the girl drowned. Still, a timeline needs to be established; they need to find out what happened. The cast and crew of the outdoor drama want to be helpful. They really do. They try. It's just that no one from the end-of-season company picnic on the river can remember, really, whether or not the girl was ever there.

Hungry

A new life. That's what it was going to be. A whole new being. I won't be her anymore, Nikki told herself. I'll be a new me. She stared at her reflection, her too-small head like a peeled onion in the bus window, repeated the words until they took on the rhythm of the humming tires beneath her, the stench of the sloshing toilet two rows behind. In Fresno her mother had handed her a twenty-dollar bill and an opened carton of cigarettes with two packs missing. It had been the sight of those two empty spaces like knocked-out teeth inside the ripped carton that caused Nikki to jerk away and climb quickly up the bus steps. She'd watched her mother on the concrete platform in her torn sweatshirt and dirty Keds, the flat, blank look of her. A cold rage sat in Nikki's chest. Her mother hadn't waved, and so she didn't; they'd just looked at each other through the smeared window, and then her mother turned to leave before the bus pulled out of the bay, and Nikki wept all the way to Bakersfield, and then she'd quit crying and the words came in her mind, *I won't be her anymore, I'll be a new me*, and she'd repeated them from Bakersfield to Barstow to Flagstaff to Albuquerque. She believed she knew what the words meant.

Sometimes she slept. Mostly she smoked cigarettes and stared at the passing desert or at her own reflected image, alien and strange, a quick nervous queasiness rippling her chest. The smell of exhaust, old urine, full ashtrays on the armrests. Two chattering Mexican women and their staring big-eyed kids. The creep in a torn suitcoat who boarded in Albuquerque and kept trying to get her to talk to him until she threatened to tell the driver and he moved a few rows up and went to sleep, and then it was Tucumcari to Amarillo in darkness, the stars low on the horizon. She drowsed awake to see a line of pink limning the earth straight ahead, swelling to fuchsia, the sky above a clear, aching blue, and for a moment her despair lifted. But full daylight revealed the flat brown emptiness of Texas, an emptiness that did not change when they crossed into Oklahoma. It was only the carved stone sign at the side of the highway that told her. Otherwise, she'd never have known—it all looked the same: flat, brown, dull, unrelenting.

The day opened full, and still it was hours before they reached the Oklahoma City bus station, where Nikki went to the snack bar and bought a Tab cola and a hot dog, but the meat gagged her, the bread gummed thick in her mouth, and she threw most of it away. She walked outside to look around. Winos in Flagstaff, winos in Gallup, winos in Albuquerque, winos here. All downtowns looked the same, she thought, except here the buildings were taller, the shadows deeper—it was almost sunset—and a biting plains wind blew paper cups and trash along the nearly empty street. A dirty, bearded man with his bottle in a paper sack sat on the sidewalk across the road, watching her. She turned and went back inside to wait for the bus to Tulsa. If she hadn't felt so heartsick she might have found it funny that a person who had been through all she'd been through would be frightened by a wino's stare.

By the time the bus pulled into the Tulsa station, the night was full dark. She saw her cousin Lyla in a pea coat and knee-high boots, her long brown hair fanned out on her shoulders, waiting on the platform beneath the purplish glare. Nikki reached for her backpack in the overhead bin, set her face to motionless as she made her way along the aisle. The instant she stepped down she heard her cousin gasp. "My God, Nikki! What happened to you?"

Instinctively she reached up to hide her head. Almost immediately she dropped her arm, lifted her chin, hoisted the dirty green backpack to her shoulder. "Let's go," she said. Her cousin glanced at the line of passengers waiting at the side of the bus for their luggage. "You didn't bring a suitcase?"

"No. Let's go," Nikki said again.

Lyla led the way through the station to the cold, dim street beyond. The wind was freezing, but it was a relief to be buffeted by air so cold it had no smell. They found the car, drove in silence through the quiet downtown streets, Nikki hunkering in her seat and shivering—she didn't own a coat—and on through a section of sparsely spaced convenience stores and small houses toward the dark, two-lane highway leading north toward the little city of Bartlesville, where her cousin's family lived. Except Lyla herself didn't live there now, Nikki remembered. She lived in some other town, going to school. The silence in the car was more than the silence of discomfort; it was the silence of distance. They'd grown up together, in summers, had been almost like sisters. Close enough to fight like sisters. But they hadn't seen each other in three years. As the car hummed north Lyla murmured, "You sure got skinny," and a short while later, "And your hair. Wow."

"Jesus, Lyla. Like you never saw a pixie cut before?"

Her cousin cut her a skeptical glance, then turned back to watch the road. It was not a pixie cut. It was a hatchet job Nikki had done herself with a butcher knife in the bedroom of her mother's apartment. This was moments after she'd been told she had two choices: get out (back to the streets the darkness the smells the helplessness hunger degradation) or go to Oklahoma, where she could stay with her aunt and uncle, who were willing, God knew why, her mother said, to take her in. In fury, without a mirror, she'd sawed off her blonde hair so close to the scalp it was hardly long enough to grasp between two fingers: a quarter inch of jagged mousy brown fuzz. "Can we turn up the heat?" She was shaking, her teeth chattering. Her cousin slid the lever hard to the right, pulled the car over and parked, shrugged out of her coat and handed it to Nikki.

"Don't you need it?"

"I'm fine," Lyla said.

"Thanks." With the warmed coat turned backwards, covering her arms and chest, Nikki's shivering began to slow. The dark countryside slid past, black rolling prairie dotted with scattered house lights, not so different at night from the San Joaquin Valley in California where Nikki grew up. Except she'd grown up here too, or anyway she'd passed through so many times on the way to and from the Tulsa airport, because in those days her mother would pay to fly her to Oklahoma for the summers. Unbidden, totally unexpected, the dark thing welled up fast, a thick hard clump in her throat that blew out in the form of ragged, gasping breaths—except she couldn't seem to catch her breath, a clamp was squeezing her chest, and she struggled to break it, struggled to breathe. This was not like the quiet weeping she'd done on the bus. This was loud and forceful, an explosion of pain. It would be years before she would come to understand that what exploded from her that night, riding in the dark car with her cousin, was grief. Years longer before she would know what she grieved.

"Nikki? Are you okay? Nik?"

"Don't. Call me that. Anymore," Nikki said between shuddering breaths.

A beat of silence. Her cousin's voice was tentative when she spoke again. "What do you want me to call you then?"

She hadn't thought that far. Had not thought until this moment, in fact, that she would need a new name, only that she was not going to be the same girl, the same person, the one who . . . her thoughts heaved into images, dark and swirling, sickening with smells: a greasy burgundy couch covered in tiny black pinpricks, the infinitesimal shit of cockroaches, their tiny dank smell blending with the sweetish smell of rotting food and the stink of the backed-up toilet overflowing from weeks of partying behind cheap lauan doors and closed blinds to block out the brittle sunlight so that no one knew if it was day or night, no one asked, because time melted into slow, warm ecstasy into vomit into shaking into ecstasy again, and the feel of men's hands, and she would swim to consciousness on the burgundy couch to feel the skimming feet of cockroaches like quicksilver racing along her thighs, her neck, her belly, and she would wipe at them, mumble to someone to turn on the light to make them go away, before she sank into blackness again, and that girl, that person, was called Nikki, and that was who she was not going to be. When she could control her breath again she said, "Call me by my name. Nicole."

"I'll try," her cousin said.

AND perhaps Lyla did try. Perhaps the sliding back into the familiar *Nikki* or *Nik* when she called to her from another room was accidental. It mattered little anyway, because Lyla left on Sunday night to drive back to college in Tahlequah, and Nikki was on her own with her aunt and uncle and weird, annoying cousin, Lyla's younger brother, Mike. Her aunt bought her a fuzzy pink mohair beret at a downtown department store, and Nikki hardly took it off in daylight, even inside the house, because Lyla's brother would stare at her goofily, stroking his own long brown locks, and ask if she wanted to borrow some.

In the daytimes she ran the vacuum cleaner for her aunt, learned how to sort laundry, memorized the names of all the characters on *The Young and the Restless*, and when that theme music came on—the

slow piano chords, the sad violins sweeping in—her chest ached with
longing. At night she'd stand in front of the bathroom mirror tug-
ging at her hair, as if that could make it grow faster, and find herself
eyeing the pocket change her uncle left on the bathroom vanity with
his keys when he went to bed. Her carton of cigarettes was long gone,
as was the twenty her mother had given her, splurged on candy bars
and Tab colas at the convenience store on the main road. Gazing at
her pale, white-lashed eyes, she'd think how washed out she looked
without mascara. She hadn't worn makeup in years, actually; it had
been disdained with such wordless contempt at the commune where
she'd lived in Sonora that she'd quit, and by the time she left the
mountains, she was used to herself without makeup. But she'd been
blonde then, and tanned, her hair long and straight and parted in
the middle. The bare bulbs above the vanity showed her skin pasty
as pie dough. The scalp job made her head look like a skull. Staring
at this person who looked nothing like her, she'd say to herself: This
is the new me I'm becoming. This is Nicole.

Her teachers at school used to call her that, and her second step-
father. When she was a very little girl, her mother called her Kiki
when she was pleased with her and Nicole May when she was not.
Why hadn't she thought to tell Lyla to call her Kiki? But then she'd
stare at her ashen face in the mirror and think: Because I'm not.

Her aunt began to ask what her plans were. "Look here," she'd say,
and hand her the evening newspaper with several want ads circled.
She'd offer to drive her to town to apply for any job she thought
might be right. At supper one night her uncle said, "People ought
to pull their own weight by the time they're your age, Nicole, don't
you think?" Her cousin Mike smirked at her from across the table.
This was the night she quietly slid two dimes and a quarter from
the pile of change on the bathroom vanity, slipped them into the
pocket of her borrowed robe. Next day, she grabbed Lyla's old brown

corduroy coat from the hall closet, walked to the convenience store and bought a pack of Marlboros.

Weeks later, drunk at a party in Tahlequah, she would realize that that was the moment she'd surrendered. Not when she smoked five cigarettes on the walk home and came in the door so nauseous and dizzy she had to go lie down, mumbling to her aunt as she passed her in the kitchen that she was too sick to set the table. Not when she began to sneak into her cousin Mike's room while he was at school to paw through his drawers looking for dope, which, whether because he hid it too cleverly or wasn't actually a head even though he looked like one, she never found. Not when she left the house in a huff one morning after her aunt·told her to come unload the dishwasher—not *later*, Nicole, *now*—and stalked to the main road leading to the highway and stuck out her thumb. Not when she showed up drunk at her cousin's dorm at eleven o'clock that night because it had seemed to her that the smartest place to stop and ask directions, once she'd hitched to Tahlequah, was the bar she'd seen lit up and full of students a block from campus. No. She'd transformed from Nicole right back into Nikki the instant those two slim dimes and one thicker quarter glided smoothly and silently beneath her two fingers along the pink Formica vanity and into her palm.

It was goody-two-shoes Lyla, of course, who insisted on calling her parents to let them know Nikki was all right—*they'll be worried half to death, Nik, you can't just leave them thinking you got kidnapped or something*—and Lyla who kept saying, *you can't stay here you can't stay here you can't stay here,* until finally she said, *okay, Thanksgiving is next week, you can stay until then.*

If Lyla had lived in a regular dorm with rules and regs and dorm mothers, it would never have worked. But Lyla lived in expanded student housing, where there were no curfew hours, no dorm mothers; the residents came and went with their own keys. At first Nikki was

just relieved. But then she thought, oh shit. Thanksgiving. Nana and
Grandpa. In her mind she saw their sad gazes, their disappointment:
how they would stare at her scalped head, her pasty skin, her bony
arms and chest, and somehow they would know. Wednesday afternoon, when Lyla hurried in from class and started packing, Nikki sat
on the unmade bed in her T-shirt and panties, smoking.

"Put that out, Nik," Lyla said. "You know it's against the rules. And
get dressed. Mom wants us to try to get there before dark."

"I'm not going."

Her cousin paused with the neck of a white crocheted sweater
tucked under her chin. "Of course you are." Lyla's tone said *don't be
stupid*. She finished folding the sweater, laid it in the blue Samsonite
suitcase opened on the foot of the bed.

"I'm not."

"They close the school, Nikki. You can't stay here."

"I'm not going."

"The cafeteria shuts down. There won't be any place to eat."

"The foreign students have to eat someplace, don't they?"

Lyla said doubtfully, "I don't think we've got any foreign students
here."

But Nikki sat on the bed with her legs drawn up, shaking her
head. Lyla mocked her; she wheedled and cajoled. She threatened
to physically pull her out of the dorm and into the car. Their grandparents would be heartbroken, she said. Finally, she exploded: "What
the hell am I supposed to tell my mom!" Nikki gazed at her without expression. "It's Thanks*giving*, Nik. Nothing in the whole town
will be open."

"I'm not going. That's all."

And in the end she didn't. In the end Lyla took two keys off her
keychain and laid them on the built-in bureau by the door. "The
one with the dab of nail polish is the front door key," she said. She

glared at Nikki from the doorway, the blue Samsonite in her hand. Then she set the suitcase down, dug in her purse, laid a five and two ones and a handful of change on the bureau next to the keys. "The café downtown will probably be open Friday," she said. "I don't know what you're going to eat tomorrow. You're on your own about that." Then she left.

Nikki rolled over and went to sleep, only to awaken in the dark a few hours later with the waves of despair rolling over her, and trembling with cold. The heat to the building had been turned off. She got up and dug through Lyla's drawers for a sweatshirt, some sweatpants, a second pair of socks. She put on her fuzzy beret, slept fitfully in and out, awakening at dawn to emptiness and hunger. For a few hours she huddled under the covers, until she couldn't stand it any longer and climbed out, put on as many layers of clothing as she could manage, grabbed the money off the bureau, and headed outside, where the temperature hovered just above freezing. The skies were gray and empty. The campus was dead. She walked to the bar where she'd stopped to ask directions a week ago, stood on the sidewalk staring at the two dark plate-glass windows. GRANNY'S ATTIC arced across both sides in matching antique letters. A hand-lettered sign taped to the door said they'd reopen for Happy Hour on Friday, November 28. Four o'clock on Friday. Jesus. More than twenty-four hours from now. Nikki walked back to the dorm, where she let herself in, used some of her cousin's change to buy a bag of Fritos and a Milky Way and a Coke from the vending machines in the basement, went to Lyla's room and huddled under the covers eating corn chips and smoking. She skimmed through one of her cousin's Special Ed textbooks till her eyes crossed, slammed the book shut, got up to pilfer through Lyla's things until she found some used makeup in the top bureau drawer—blue eye shadow, frosted pink lipstick, a cake of black Maybelline eyeliner that you drew on with a tiny wet brush like a watercolor.

The next afternoon, her hunger only slightly assuaged by more chips and candy bars, she sat at her cousin's desk with the makeup mirror lit, drawing thin perfect black lines on her eyelids and under her lower lashes, winging them out to the sides in tiny dramatic swooshes like Liz Taylor in *Cleopatra*. She darkened her face with beige base from a nearly empty bottle of CoverGirl, wrapped a paisley scarf she'd found in the closet around her head and tied it to one side behind her ear. She gazed at herself with pleasure. This was the change she'd been seeking. A new outside to reflect a new inside. A new person altogether. A new life. She tugged on her cousin's boots, a half-size too small, and Lyla's denim jacket, not nearly warm enough, and walked to Granny's Attic.

It might have been Happy Hour, but there was nothing very happy about the place. It was a strange bar anyway, in that it had no bar to sit at, only a lit cubbyhole where you stood to order your beer. Everything else was tables, small round four-tops and large wooden industrial spools turned on their sides and covered with checkered oilcloth, surrounded by six or eight wooden chairs. There was nobody here, or anyways nothing like the noisy crowd she'd joined the night she arrived in Tahlequah. Two redneck guys sat in the back sharing a pitcher, and a young couple who looked like high schoolers held hands and made kissy face by the door. At a large spool table in the far right-hand corner sat a shaggy-looking longhair with a half-empty pitcher and a slim-bodied Coors glass in front of him. His face showed no surprise when Nikki stood across from him with two full glasses in hand—two-for-one draws and buck-fifty pitchers: Happy Hour—and said, "Mind if I sit?"

He gestured with his open palm to the chair beside him. Nikki took the next one over. "You expecting company?" she asked, indicating the half dozen other empty chairs. "You," the guy said. She peered at him. He seemed kind of familiar. "How's that?" she asked.

The guy shrugged, tossed his head slightly in a way that flipped his shaggy bangs out of his eyes. "I was waiting for somebody," he said. "Appears you're the one who showed up."

"Is that right?"

"That is right." He drank his beer. She studied him. His face was long, dark, his cheeks faintly nicked with old acne scars, his hair black and shiny and cut in a shag, or grown out into one, and he was slim as a bird. He had on a denim jacket over a white T-shirt. He looked Mexican. Or not Mexican, she thought. Indian. Like that kid in her grandparents' town when she was growing up—Hubert, Hulbert, whatever his name was. Maybe that's why he seemed familiar.

"This is one boring town," she said. "You ever see a place so boring?"

"Yes," he said. She waited for him to say more, but he didn't.

"Well, I haven't," Nikki said. "Not this bad. Jesus." She could just make out her reflection, far away, dreamy seeming in the dim plate-glass window. Not an onion head, she thought. A gypsy. A wild-hearted vagabond. "So," she said. "What's your story?"

"What's yours?"

"No, I mean, how come you're here?"

He raised his brows, lowered them, took a sip of beer as if pondering this profoundest of questions.

"I mean, you live here or what?" she said.

His gaze took in the nearly empty bar. His tone was flat, ironical, when he said, "Isn't it pretty to think so."

"But you're a student, right?"

"Nominally."

"A foreign student?"

He barked a laugh.

"Well, I mean, how come you're here when nobody else in the freaking world is?"

"My roommates went home for Thanksgiving. I didn't."

"Why not?"

He looked at her very somberly. In a serious, reserved tone, he said, "Indians don't celebrate Thanksgiving."

"Oh. Sorry." She was flustered, embarrassed. She was from California. What did she know about Indians? Then the guy said, "*Aaaaay*," a low, guttural, drawn-out sound, and started laughing, and she knew he'd been joking. She got even more flustered, and not a little pissed off. "That's cheap, man," she said. But she let it go. "So, seriously, what's your story?"

"I'll tell you mine if you tell me yours." But immediately he leaned over and emptied the last of his pitcher into her glass, stood up. "Want to split another?" He threaded his way to the cubbyhole, returned with two pitchers and a couple of packages of Slim Jims. "Supper," he said in that dry, flat tone, opened the packages and divided four skinny wizened sausages between them. He raised his glass in a toast. "Here's to friendship between our peoples, thine and mine, that we may feed one another and offer libations and song and enduring friendship as long as the grass shall grow and the waters run, or until you annihilate us all—whichever comes first."

"Jesus," Nikki said. But the beer on her empty stomach was starting to take effect. "We," she said, gesturing between them, "are dressed just alike." He looked down at his jeans and jean jacket, over at hers. Then he narrowed his eyes at the scarf on her head. "I don't have a bandana."

"We'll get you one."

He raised his glass. "I'll drink to that."

"To bandanas," she said and lifted her glass. "I'll drink to the total boringness of this day, when all the world is fed up on turkey and tired of giving thanks."

"Except us," he said.

"Except us." They drank.

"A toast," the guy said, "to deflated balloons, deflated egos, deflation
in all its purest and most wondrous forms, which are sorely needed
in these our hallowed days of inflation as the total norm."

"Deflated balloons?"

"Macy's Thanksgiving Day Parade."

"Oh. Right," she said. "I'll drink to that." They drank. "Here's to
new friendships."

"And old ones." They drank. "What's your name, new old friend?"
he said.

She hesitated. Kiki? Or something more exotic. Natasha, perhaps.
"I'll tell you mine if you tell me yours."

"Floyd," he said. "Floyd Sixkiller."

"Floyd *Six Killer!*" She started laughing, then stopped. "You're shit-
ting, right?" He didn't answer. "Oh. Okay. Sorry." Probably it was for
this reason alone—her baffled embarrassment, the unhappy sense
she'd hurt his feelings—that she told him the simple truth: her name
was Nikki. No embellishment. No dramatification at all.

By the end of the night, they'd spent most of Nikki's money and
all of Floyd's. They'd learned what they had in common—a secret
liking for the voice of Karen Carpenter, for instance, which they both
would have croaked before admitting to anyone else (the songs are
so *hokey*, Nikki said, and Floyd said, oh God, and those ka-thumping
drums!; he did a slow, plodding tom-tom run on the tabletop. But
her voice is really sweet, Nikki said, and Floyd said, sweet enough to
cut your heart out, and Nikki said, yes, and Floyd said, yes, and then
he leaned over and whispered, if you ever tell a soul I said that, I'll
have to cut *your* heart out, and Nikki mimed locking her lips, and
they lifted their beers, toasted their secret)—and also what they did
not share: a sense of home.

Of all the swoops and swirls in their conversation, the darting in
and out, the tumbling recognitions one on top of the other, that was

the only turn that made Nikki uncomfortable. It was the second of two questions Floyd asked that she didn't know how to answer. The first, drawled in the flat, dry voice that she now recognized meant he was joking, was: what do you want to be when you grow up? This she couldn't answer because, in fact, she had not thought about it since childhood. For years now, half her life, really, she had wanted nothing except to have a good time; she hadn't thought about *being* anything. She spilled out the same answer she used to give grown-ups when they asked her that as a child: "A beautiful ballerina."

"Score!" Floyd cried, clinking his glass to hers. "Me too!"

Nikki went *aaaay!* in just the way Floyd did, the two of them drawing out the syllable at the same time, laughing. They went through the usual lists—favorite bands, singers, foods, colors, movies, songs, beers, actors—and they matched in an astonishing number of categories and argued extravagantly when they disagreed. The evening advanced, the park across the street filled with shadows, but the lights inside the bar were golden and warm. A handful of other drinkers came in, longhairs and rednecks, a few hippie chicks, but Nikki and Floyd were separate, wrapped in their own world, their corner table, lifted above. The beer loosened their gestures, their tongues. Nikki knew they were getting loud. She could feel others staring at them. They're jealous, she thought. We are golden. And that is how she felt: golden. She felt comfortable and easy. She felt as if she'd known Floyd Sixkiller all her life.

"Did you ever feel like you're living your life backwards?" she asked.

Floyd pondered the question, squinting a little, tilting his head to the side. This was one of the things she liked about him—he didn't knee-jerk anything. He really considered. She also liked how the faint little scars on his cheeks made him seem older but the way he shrugged the hair out of his eyes made him seem young. She liked how long and slim his fingers were when he reached across and drew a cigarette out of her pack on the table. "What do you mean?" he said.

"Like, you know, shit will happen, and you'll realize later you knew it was going to happen, but you didn't know you knew till after it happened."

"Oh. Yeah," he said, nodding. "That."

"You know what I'm talking about?"

"I do." Floyd took her cigarette from her hand to light his own.

"One time," she said, "me and these other freaks I was living with in Sonora, we were tripping on mescaline at this place way up in the Sierras, somebody's land up above Twain Harte. There were like four of us, and we were sitting beside this pond, the sun was burning down you wouldn't believe how hot, because we were naked and it was really high up, you know, and nobody was talking, we were all just tripping on these amazing patterns in the water, and at some point, way down the mountain, on the road, like about a mile away, this car horn sounded. Just once, like, *hoonnk!*, that's it, and then all this time passed, an hour or something, and I went, Oh, wow, because I realized I knew that was going to happen, it was *supposed* to happen. And when I looked up, the others were all looking at me. Everybody was nodding because we all knew that was going to happen. You know? We all knew it. And this one chick smiles at me with her eyes closed, like the Buddha, like that laughing Buddha, you've seen it?" Floyd nodded, but then he shrugged. Nikki wanted to tell him how that car horn was a sign, how it was a part of the great invisible cosmic orchestration, because the next day that same girl's sister came in a car to take her home to Tuolumne, and Nikki went with them, and that was how she left Sonora, where she'd been living almost a year, and returned to her mother's house in Visalia, and that had been a good thing, that first time, going back to her mother's. Until it wasn't anymore. But it all seemed too hard to explain. She shook her head, reached for his hand to take back her cigarette. "So," she said, shrugging, "I went home."

"What is that?" he said.

"What's what?"

"Home."

And here it was, the second question she couldn't answer—one she didn't even have a flippant quip for. The very word filled her with discomfort, like the jittery nausea she'd felt on the bus ride from California, but the feeling was mixed with a vague, impossible longing, like an ache for something she'd lost but never really had. It was the same feeling she'd get in her aunt's living room when the violins swept in over the piano chords at the opening of *The Young and the Restless*. The word did not evoke the town of Visalia, where she'd spent her early teen years hating every goddamn minute and every inch of the place, or the crummy little apartment in Fresno where her mother had moved last year after her last divorce. It didn't evoke Sonora, Oakland, Santa Cruz, the half dozen other places she'd lived since she ran away from her mother's house at sixteen, and it surely, surely, oh, God, did not evoke the flophouse with the greasy burgundy couch in East L.A. where she'd ended up nearly dying before crawling to Fresno last summer to beg her mother to take her in. Nikki looked at the dark large window across the room, her tiny, wrapped head reflected as if on the other side, the golden lights in this room, the beer buzz chatter all around. She threw her head back, swept one arm in a grand inclusive gesture to take in the world. "I'm a vagabond! Can't you tell? Home is wherever I drop my backpack!"

Floyd went on gazing at her, his eyes narrowed, his face serious in a way she hadn't yet seen—not set with that mock, dry seriousness that meant he was pulling her leg, but somber serious, dead serious, like his question might be the most significant question in the world. "You don't know, do you?" he said.

"I told you. I don't have one. I'm a wild, gypsy-girl vagabond!"

"Not *where* it is," Floyd said softly. "*What* it is."

She was suddenly terrified. "Hell, yes, I know," she said. "It's . . . like where you frigging grew up! Or something." Floyd waited. "Well, hell, I can't describe it! All right, Mister Oh-So-Wise, you tell me."

He drew in a slow breath, rolled the tip of his cigarette against the ashtray. After a beat he said, "It's where the Creator set you to be. The trees he set for your people, or the desert where there aren't any trees. The angle of the moon there. The scent of rain on that earth." She waited for him to show he was joking. He was not joking.

"I don't guess I have any people," she said. "Much less someplace God set me to be."

"You do," he said. "You don't have to know it. And I didn't say God. I said Creator."

"Whatever," she shrugged. And then: "Oh, what—you mean like the Great Spirit or some shit?"

Floyd stood, walked away toward the men's room. The fear clamped down around her. She weaved her way to the cubbyhole, ordered another pitcher. When Floyd came back she apologized, but he only ducked his head, waved his hands, and shrugged. "No, man," she insisted. "I really am sorry. I am. I'm going to learn to keep my goddamn stupid mouth shut. Anyway, that's not what I meant to say. I meant to say, how do you know? How do you find it if your people left it in the first place?"

"Not like it was their choice."

"Yeah. But I mean, how do you know?"

"It's here," he said, and he made the most elegant gesture. He stretched out his hand, turned his wrist up, the long delicate shape of it protruding from the cuff of denim, his brown smooth skin lifted skyward, the intricacy of veins showing in the dim light. "Here's where I remember." He paused. "Even if she don't," he said softly, "I do."

"Who?"

Floyd shrugged, flipped his hair. Then, as if to shift the subject, as if to keep the thing he'd started to say sealed tight inside, he let loose the low guttural sound, *aaaay*, and Nikki joined him. But it was not the same as before.

The bar closed. She went home with him. *Home*, it turned out, was a cramped one-bedroom apartment in a low redbrick building north of campus. A jumble of beanbag chairs and milk crates, crumpled food sacks, empty beer cans, full ashtrays, a woven vinyl lawn chair, and a foldout couch splayed open, two sleeping bags for covers, one pillow. The door to the bedroom was closed. "Shh," Floyd whispered with a dramatic gesture. "Best not wake the dragons." In the kitchen a big metal pot of congealed beans sat on the stove. They ate the beans with spoons directly from the pot, shared the last can of Schlitz Floyd fished out of the fridge. In the narrow bathroom, Nikki squeezed out a line of Pepsodent, brushed her teeth with her finger. When she came back to the front room, Floyd was already asleep on the hide-a-bed, curled up in one of the sleeping bags. He'd left the pillow on top of the other sleeping bag for her. She lay down beside him. The light was still on in the kitchen, the radio turned very low, Marty Balin's yearning croon pleading for someone to believe like he believes . . . Nikki wrapped the smoky-smelling green cocoon around herself, drifted toward sleep. She'd almost never felt so content.

AND so, she stayed. Floyd's roommates turned out to be a couple of Native guys from Tonkawa and Pawhuska who slept in the twin beds in the bedroom and accepted Nikki's presence as wordlessly as Floyd did. She had a big fight with her cousin when she returned her boots and jean jacket, but then Lyla-the-Wuss said she could keep the jacket till she got a coat of some kind. Not the boots though.

"No problem," Nikki said, perched on the edge of the bed, lacing her sneakers. "They don't fit anyway."

"What are you going to do? I mean, how are you going to live? Nana is so worried. Mom told her what you did."

Nikki's heart clenched. *What you did what you did what you did . . .* Her grandmother's devastated gaze. The sorrowing love there. But then she realized Lyla just meant how she'd run off from her aunt's house. "I'll get a job," Nikki said.

"Who's going to hire a high school dropout in a town full of college kids looking for work?"

Nikki stood up, walked out of the room; she did not see or speak to her cousin again for many months. But at Floyd's house, things were good. She tried to make herself useful. She'd pick up the crushed beer cans, empty the ashtrays, take out the trash. She wanted them to want her around, and they seemed to, especially after she got her night job stocking shelves at Wal-Mart and started bringing home bread and bologna and beer. The apartment was nothing like the places she'd lived before—the various communes with their *oh, wow, man, far-out* judgments, the grade schools and junior highs where she'd never fit. She didn't fit at the L.A. flophouse either, even though she'd shot as much dope as the rest of them, but she always knew, waking in the night with the roaches crawling, the shakes coming, and the sickness: she knew she was different. Not better, exactly. Not *more* than. But she wanted more. She wanted . . . beauty. To look at it. To breathe it.

She and Floyd went to the bar sometimes when they had money, but mostly they bought cheap beer on sale and partied at home. She felt good there, at Floyd's apartment. It was always a party, always laughter, always a bunch of people in and out, lots of cigarette smoke and beer and sometimes sweet wine, but no dope, no hard liquor, and Nikki could handle wine and beer. She laughed when they laughed, though half the time she didn't know what they were laughing about. There was always some inside joke she couldn't figure, but the thing was, they didn't exclude her. It was like *contempt* wasn't in their vocabulary, like they knew who she was, who they were, who everybody was, and it was all good.

And Floyd. Floyd, man. He was her brother. Late at night, after the parties died down and it was just her and him sitting cross-legged on the hide-a-bed, smoking, talking, they'd share stories, things they'd never told anyone. What hurt so bad when they were little. What didn't. What they wanted more than anything.

Turned out Floyd wasn't lying when he said he wanted to be a beautiful ballerina. Or a beautiful dancer, anyway. There was no dance program at the college, but Floyd's sister in Tulsa paid for his dance classes at a studio in town. Nikki kept pestering until finally he agreed to let her come watch. She stood in the dim hallway and looked through the open door at all the pretty white girls in leotards leaping across the floor and Floyd in the midst of them, a head taller, two shades darker, a hundred times more graceful, and that was when she knew. How it was that she and Floyd meshed. Where they touched. They weren't alike because they were both misfits who'd been pushed to the outside till they found their right inside. No. They were alike because they had the same hunger. For Floyd, it was hunger to be beauty, in his body, to dance beauty. For Nikki, it was visual. She wanted to *see* beauty. Take it in through her eyes. And Floyd was beautiful, and the campus was beautiful with its clear brook gurgling along the border and its arched and turreted brick building like a castle, and even Nikki herself was beautiful, with her beige hair growing out and her black-winged eyeliner and the crop tops and hip-hugger bellbottoms she smuggled out of Wal-Mart under her shirt.

Still, she *wanted*. She just couldn't say what. The feeling wasn't there

in the daytime, or in the late-night golden hours of beer buzz and
stories. Only later, after Floyd had fallen asleep and she'd lie awake
listening to the radio. It wasn't enough to see beauty, she understood.
She had to capture it hold it express it—or express the loss of it: how
she felt when she watched the winter sun going down or, like now,
lying in the dark listening to some singer's sweet voice, a saxophone
riff, a piano, her heart aching like it could crack.

She started sketching pictures of Floyd while he slept, or she'd draw
pictures of the bare trees in the park, the front windows of Granny's
Attic, using ballpoint pen on lined paper she stole from Floyd's school
notebooks. He would have given her the paper if she'd asked, but she
didn't want him to see the drawings because they weren't any good.
She'd work half an hour or an hour when nobody was looking, trying to make her lines match what she saw, but they never matched.
She'd end up crumpling the pages into little balls and stuffing them
under the food scraps and beer cans in the kitchen trash. Maybe if I
could paint it, she thought. She stole a plastic box of kid's watercol-
ors from her job—bright primary colors, two tiny thin brushes—but
painting didn't work any better. She threw the box and brushes away.

Spring deepened. The small reddish tree buds opened into rus-
tling chartreuse whispers that turned into dark, rich, hunter green
clumps, each leaf notched and lobed like a hand. So different from
California. There, the naked trunks of palm trees marched straight
ahead in uniform rows above bougainvillea planted along the free-
ways to counter the smog, which of course it never could. Here, the
oaks and sycamores spread their chaotic shadows over the town
brook like a benediction. Here, the insects hummed, the birds sang,
the breezes kissed your face, and everything felt like a promise, like
something was coming, the sleeping world was unfolding, the future
you'd been waiting for all winter was now.

Then Floyd started rehearsals for a spring dance recital and was gone most nights. He'd get home just as Nikki was leaving for work. There were no parties at the apartment anymore, or very few, only on the weekends. And her job at Wal-Mart was boring as hell. They treated her like a criminal. Well, they treated everyone that way, like they expected every employee to steal from them. Which just made Nikki want to steal more. Which she did. But she never got caught. She was good at stealing. Still, she was restless, antsy. This was not how it was supposed to be.

Sometimes she'd see her cousin at a distance when she cut through campus on her way to work or to the bar. Lyla always waved. Nikki always acted like she didn't see. She went to a powwow one night with one of the roommates, Jim Ed. It was held inside a school gym and didn't look like she'd expected a powwow to look. Not that she could have said what that was, really. Just something less . . . present-day, she guessed. People of all ages filled the bleachers or sat on folding chairs rimming the gym floor, and a ring of drummers in cowboy hats and ball caps pounded a giant drum in the middle and sang songs that made Nikki's heart beat hard and fast, and everyone moved in a circle, the little kids and men and boys and young girls and women in shawls stepping, stepping, in an endless circle beneath the bright gymnasium lights. Jim Ed left her sitting by herself way up high in the bleachers while he went down to dance, and Nikki felt totally weird and out of place. She left and walked home. When she stopped at QuikTrip to buy a six-pack, she used the pay phone outside to call in sick to work.

That night she asked Floyd why he didn't go to powwows and do Indian dances instead of taking ballet and modern, which weren't Indian at all. Obviously.

"You don't think Indians can dance like white folks?"

"No, I mean—no. I was just curious."

"Don't be."

She looked at him. He was just out of the shower, his black hair combed back wet so that when he ticked his head, his bangs didn't flip to the side. He was rolling the tip of his cigarette against the ashtray. "I didn't grow up in it," he said without looking up.

"In what? Powwows?"

The way he shrugged could have been a yes, could've been a no.

"But you grew up taking ballet lessons?"

"You think all Indians are alike."

"No. I don't know. How would I know?"

"Exactly," Floyd said.

That shut her up for a while. In a bit she asked if he wanted a beer. Floyd nodded, and she went to the kitchen. When she came back, the TV was on: an old John Wayne movie, a western, no sound. They pulled the tabs on their beer cans, sat watching as silent Indians on horseback swept across a river, their painted faces contorted as they yelled their silent yells, and John Wayne stood tall on the far bank, aiming his silent, puffing rifle, picking them off one by one.

"Why are we watching this?" Nikki said.

"Makes me laugh."

"You're not laughing."

"Inside I am," Floyd said. He sipped his beer. On the screen, dying warriors fell silently off their horses into the roiling water. "They're missing the one where the Indian gets shot off his horse but his foot's caught so the horse drags him. I thought that was *de rigeur*."

"What?"

"Obligatory."

"You think you're so smart."

"Indians can't be smart either?"

She cut him a look. "What's with this Indians can or can't shit?"

"You started it."

"How?"

He made his voice deep, held his palm flat toward her. "How, Kee-mo-sah-bee!"

"Quit!"

Floyd was laughing now. She snatched up the pillow and whacked him. Floyd crossed his arms dramatically over his head. "I'm not into S and M!" he shouted, still laughing. "Quit, bitch. You're going to make me spill my beer!"

"Good enough for you, sucker!" Nikki was laughing too.

"Kill the Indian, save the child!"

Nikki quit hitting him. "Why are you like this tonight?"

"Why are you?"

"I'm not like anything. You are."

"Oh, right." He made his voice high and feminine. "'Why don't you dance like an Indian, Floyd? Why do you do *pliés* with white girls? Why aren't you a dumb Indian like you're supposed to be?'"

"I didn't say that!"

"'Why are you such a faggot?'"

"Floyd! I didn't say that! I don't care, you know I don't care!"

"Maybe you don't. The whole rest of the world does."

"Not your friends! Not Jim Ed and Raymond! Not everybody who hangs out here!"

He got stone quiet. "What makes you think they know?"

Nikki didn't have an answer. She'd known Floyd was gay the night they met, even before she came home with him and he didn't try to screw her. She couldn't even say why she knew. It was just how it was. Why wouldn't his friends know? But then she thought, probably they do; he just thinks they don't. Or wants to think so. Anyway, it wasn't something anybody talked about. On the muted television John Wayne swaggered across the screen in his red shirt and yellow kerchief and sweat-stained brown hat. "You know what?" Nikki said. "I am sick of looking at that son of a bitch." She got up and turned off the TV. Then the room was more silent than ever. "So," she said. "What happened tonight?"

Floyd flapped his hand, a dismissal. "Just the usual. Just the director telling me to quit making my *jetés* so *grand*. She means quit showing up the white girls whose daddies pay for her classes. It's going to suck. The whole recital. I don't want anyone to see it. We look like a bunch of frigging amateurs."

"Then don't go," Nikki said. "Don't try to be one of them. You're not. You're a thousand times better. Why do you want to go where you don't belong?"

"I could say the same to you."

Nikki looked at him, frowning.

"You hang out with us trying to act all Native, all *aaay* and *ennit* and fake turquoise jewelry. You laugh at our jokes like you know what's funny."

"No I don't!"

"And now you're going to powwows," Floyd said. "Give me a break."

"I didn't stay!"

"Because why?"

"Because it was boring!"

"And you want to know why I don't dance powwow?"

"You think it's boring too?"

"No." It was almost a whisper. "I do not." He jabbed out his cigarette. "You don't know what it means when I say I didn't grow up in it."

"So tell me."

"I grew up in fucking West Tulsa, Nikki. Where I got chased down by white boys every goddamn day. That's how I got so good at *chassé*." He laughed. "My stepdad was a white-ass son of a bitch who would've croaked before he let us go to a powwow, or anything like it."

"Not new news," Nikki said. Floyd had talked about his stepdad a lot. Another place their lives matched—hated stepfathers. In Nikki's case there were several. In Floyd's case, only one. But he hated him with a white-hot passion fierce enough to match Nikki's four.

He sat quiet a beat. Then he shrugged. "I didn't grow up Cherokee, that's all. My mom, she—" He broke off. His face closed. "Forget it," he said. He slid off the sofa bed, went to the kitchen for more beer. His face was different when he came back, all animated and exaggeratedly happy, like he'd thrown off a curtain. "This is the last one." He pulled off the ring tab and dropped it in the ashtray, handed the can to Nikki for the first sip. "So, tell me, Miss Thang. What's the naughtiest thing you ever done?" This was their old game, comparing their pasts: worst, best, scariest, stupidest, smartest, wickedest, wildest—they constantly changed the descriptors.

"We already did that one." Nikki drank, handed him back the can.

"What was it?"

"Rubbed pepper sauce on my mom's diaphragm."

Floyd shrieked. "Oh, that's gorgeous!" He narrowed his eyes. "What if you were lying?"

"I wasn't."

"What if *I* was?"

"Were you?"

"Hell, I don't know." They laughed. "All right. If you could live anywhere in the world, with all the money in the world, where would it be?"

"New York," Nikki said immediately. Not that she had any particular ambition to live in New York—it was just the farthest you could get from California. And California was where she never wanted to be again. "You?"

"Paris, my love." He struck an elegant pose. "Gay P*ah*ree!" He made the *ahr* guttural in his throat. "The French love us Indians."

"How do you know that?"

"I just know." Floyd drank, handed her the beer. "Your turn."

"Okay." She didn't know how to say it, but it was the thing that crushed her. "What's . . . the . . . secret of your heart? The thing you crave but can never tell anyone."

"To be Maria Tallchief!"

"No, I'm serious. I mean, like something you want so bad, you'd give anything for it. Even when you know it's impossible."

"You think being the most perfect ballerina in the world is easy?" He laughed, but when Nikki sat waiting with a somber look on her face, he said, "I want to fly."

She made a little *tsk* sound, handed him the can. "That's not hard. Join the Air Force or something."

"Not that way. Not in a machine. I want to fly like in my dreams. Like, I'll take a long, high leap across a dark field, then another, and another, and with each leap, gravity holds me less, and a little less. And then on the last one, I'm skimming over the earth, just gliding, with these rolling green hills flying by below—not far below, only a dozen yards or so. And the light is glowing, like that low slant of sun underneath clouds, and it's pure . . . ecstasy. It's perfection. No weight to hold me." He turned to look at her. "But not in my dreams, girl. For real."

"Yeah," she breathed. "I get that."

"Last sip," he said and gave her the beer. "What's yours?"

"I want . . ." She drained the can, crumpled it, set it on the crowded end table. "Oh, man. It sounds so hokey."

"Hokier than wanting to fly?"

"I want to, like . . . be an artist, I think."

"So be one."

"I can't draw."

"Don't let that stop you."

"I got no freaking talent, Floyd! I can't draw, I can't paint, I can't dance, I can't sing—"

"Don't be an artist then. Be a maker. Make stuff because you like it. You can do anything you want—cook, sew, pick up trash. Be beautiful in your everydayness."

"You don't get it! I want . . . when I feel . . . when my chest hurts and my throat aches and I feel like I could crawl out of my skin, or I want to run, run hard, run fast, run away, I want . . ." She sat heaving, tears running down. "When I see what's beautiful, and I can't even say it."

"Practice," Floyd said. "That's what I do."

A bolt of anger flashed through her. Floyd didn't get it either. Not even him. Nobody got it. She was on her own. She could flail around stupid and ignorant her whole freaking life working at Wal-Mart for $2.10 an hour till she got old and ugly and croaked. Who cared? Suddenly she jumped up. "Let's dance!" She went to the windowsill and turned on the radio.

"Oh God," Floyd groaned as the music came on; he wilted against the cushions like he was melting. "The Captain and Tennille! We can't dance to that shit."

"No." Nikki was laughing now—or pretending to. "We absolutely cannot." She reached for Floyd's hand to pull him up off the couch.

SHE quit her job. Or she didn't so much quit it as quit going—after that night, she never went back. She didn't go pick up her last check. It was only for one shift anyway. She told herself it wasn't worth the trouble. Really, she just didn't want to look at them, the manager, the other stockers. She told Floyd she was going to get a job at the health food store downtown, or maybe the bakery. And she did go by there, both places. But they didn't need any help.

She started walking Floyd to class in the mornings, then sometimes she'd go around town asking in stores if they had any openings, but mostly she hung out in the little park across the street from

Granny's Attic smoking and dreaming till Floyd finished class. She'd meet him when he came out of Seminary Hall or the science building, walk him to the maintenance plant, where he clocked in for his afternoon work-study job; then she'd follow him around helping him clean the restrooms, run the floor polisher in the student union. One afternoon as they emptied trash into the giant dumpster behind the ad building, he asked her to come to his dress rehearsal that night.

"I'll come to the real thing."

"No. I don't want you to. If it's as shitty as I think it's going to be, I'm going to have to slit my wrists."

"No you're not."

"Just come tell me if it's awful."

That evening she sat in the auditorium at the community center with a handful of anxious mothers and watched Floyd trying to contain himself, pulling in his arms at the elbows instead of stretching them their full length, taking mincing *chassé* steps. Even at that, he was the best dancer on the stage. He was the only male, the only Indian. It hurt to watch.

Afterwards, a photographer hired to do publicity photos started directing the dancers where to stand, how to pose. He'd peer into his viewfinder, turn a little knob on the camera to focus, wave his hand this way or that: that's good, sweetheart, beautiful, *click,* there you go, that's it, hold it! *click, click.* He had the dancers line up behind the skinny young prima ballerina, told her to do an arabesque. "Good, good, that's it, gorgeous!" he called out. *Click, click, click, click.* His vinyl camera bag sat unattended on a padded chair in the second row. Nikki slipped over, opened it, pawed around inside. No extra cameras like she'd hoped, just some round clunky lenses and a half dozen rolls of film secured with elastic under the lid. She took one roll of film, slipped it into her jeans pocket. She picked up one of the capped lenses, but it was too big to hide in a pocket, so she put it back. She moved to the foot of the stage. Standing behind the photographer, she made a frame with her hands, thumb to thumb, palms squared like facing *L*'s. Everybody was so preoccupied with posing, nobody was paying attention to her. Except Floyd, who was dying with suppressed laughter. She framed him, squinted, closed one eye, mouthed, *that's it, gorgeous—beautiful, sweetheart!* Floyd did a perfect arabesque, his long fingers extended, delicate as bird bones, his hair shining black under the stage lights. "No, no, no! Stand still, kid!" the photographer shouted. "You're messing up the shot!"

"So?" Floyd said later when they were sitting at Granny's with a full pitcher between them. "What did you think?"

"I think you're exquisite."

"I don't have to slit my wrists?"

"You do not."

"But what about the rest of it, I mean the whole evening. Amateur City, right?"

"What do you care?"

"I might invite somebody to come. But not if it's excruciating."

"Who?"

"Just tell me—would you invite somebody you cared about to come see that mess? If it was you up there, I mean."

"You've got a crush! You turkey, why didn't you tell me?"

"It's not that. It's just . . . sometimes you just have to prove something to somebody."

"Who?"

"None of your beeswax. I'll tell you if they come." He reached for his cigarettes.

"No, it's good, Floyd. You're good. Invite them." She didn't want to tell him how starkly he stood out: so much taller, darker, stronger— he dwarfed the other dancers. And he wasn't going to be in any of the publicity photos either, she didn't think. After the arabesque, the photographer had motioned Floyd to the end of the row and never aimed his camera that far. Nikki had watched him. She hated the fucker. She wished now she'd taken more than one roll of film. She reached into her pocket and took out the roll, picked at the end tab and began to unspool the film.

"Where did you get that? Oh, my God." Floyd started to laugh. They both laughed as she pulled out the entire exposed roll, scooped the film into a small black pile on the red-and-white checkered oilcloth.

"Bye-bye, little white girls," Nikki sang. "Hey. Maybe I'll become a photographer. That's art, right? Sort of."

"You could, sure, once you get a job so you can buy yourself a camera and lots of film and rent a darkroom or pay to get your film developed, and *after* you pay your part of the groceries and rent which, I remind you—and this only at the behest of our shy fellow roommates—is overdue."

"I'm looking!" she said.

"Don't look. Get."

"When did you decide to be such a bore?"

He laughed, poured them both another draft. "When Jim Ed started dunning me for your part of the rent."

"He didn't!"

"He did."

"That bitch. Wait till I get to New York and become a famous photographer! I'll smear his ugly mug all over *Mad* magazine."

"You'll have to learn to draw then."

"Whatever. Give me a cigarette."

TURNED out her cousin Lyla was right, though. It wasn't so easy getting a job in a college town, especially if you didn't have any references—she wasn't about to use the Wal-Mart manager—and who would've thought you needed a high school diploma to work at Pizza Hut? Or Sonic, for that matter. But apparently you did, because that question was always on the applications. Even after Nikki started putting down that she'd graduated Visalia High School in 1972, she still didn't get any callbacks. Well, probably not having a phone at the apartment didn't help.

One morning she woke up with an especially bad hangover to see Floyd sitting against the back of the sofa bed, smoking, staring at nothing. Nikki fumbled a smoke out of the pack on the end table, reached for Floyd's hand to pull his cigarette over to light hers. He took his hand away, swung his legs off the bed, went down the hall to the bathroom, and shut the door. She waited for him to come out so she could ask what had got his tail over a crack, and also so she could pee, but he was taking forever, so she tugged on some cutoffs, pulled a dollar bill out of Floyd's jeans crumpled on the beanbag chair, and walked up the road to the gas station. She used their filthy restroom, bought two tallboys—one for her and one for Floyd—but the apartment was empty when she got back, so she drank both. The beer eased her headache, got the day started, and she pushed that cigarette moment out of her head.

But it kept happening. Floyd pulling away. Sometimes it was physical, like how he'd take his hand back when she reached for his smoke or his beer. Other times it was silence: not talking, not listening, not staying up late to tell stories. What did I do? she thought. I didn't do shit.

And then she thought maybe that was it. What she didn't do. Like, get a job. Don't I try, though? Well, apparently not hard enough. She would try harder. Every single day, every store in town, every fast food place, and she would get hold of some money somehow and give it to Floyd; she'd stop mooching his food and beer and smokes. That wasn't Floyd's word, *mooch*. It's what the hippies in Sonora called her when she didn't have money or food or dope to contribute to the communal pot, which was most times, which was half the reason she went home to Visalia to her mother's house, but Floyd never said anything about mooching. He said very little at all, in fact. Only one night, near the end of the semester, when she kept asking what was wrong and he kept saying, *nothing* and *you wouldn't understand* and *forget about it* and *just leave it, okay?* But she couldn't leave it, she was drowning, she kept prodding until Floyd flew into a flapping rage: "For God's sake, Nikki, not everything in the freaking world is about you!" He flounced out of the apartment and didn't come home that night. When he did, he was more quiet and distant than ever. And Nikki still didn't have a job.

She went to the campus one hot, bright May afternoon and waited outside her cousin's dorm. She'd brought Lyla's jean jacket as a pretext for visiting, though it was doubtful Lyla needed it now. The sun was piercing, and blistery as hell. When she saw Lyla strolling toward her from the parking lot, Nikki jumped up, brushed off her shorts, quickly ran her hands through her hair. "Hey, cuz!" she said lightly as if no time or trouble had passed.

"Wow," Lyla said. "Look at you."

"What?" Nikki looked down at herself. Her front-tied crop top was clean enough, surely.

"Nothing. Just . . . I wasn't sure you were still in town."

"I am."

"Okay."

"I brought you this." Nikki held out the jacket. "I know it's hot already and everything, but I figured, you know. Anyway, I don't need it." Lyla took the jacket, but she didn't ask Nikki to come inside. There were a few awkward minutes where neither said anything. Finally, Lyla said, "Your hair grew out."

Nikki reached up, tugged a strand. "Yeah."

"Well," Lyla said, "I got to go pack." She started up the steps. "I'll tell Nana I saw you."

"Pack for where?"

"Home. Semester's over."

"Oh, right."

"Just for a week. Then I'm going to Indiana."

"Indiana. Wow." Nikki had a sinking feeling. "What for?"

"I got a job."

"Oh."

Lyla paused on the steps, peering down at Nikki with her hand flattened over her eyes for shade. "You're welcome to come home with me if you want."

"Why would I want to do that?"

Lyla shrugged, turned to pull open the heavy door.

"Wait!" Nikki didn't know how to keep her. "I mean, isn't your mom mad at me?"

"Not really. I told them you're doing okay. Said you're working. Are you? I mean, I guess you must be." She glanced down at Nikki's feet. "I like your sandals."

"You can have them." Nikki stepped out of the stolen leather sandals, tried to hand them to her cousin by the straps. "Payback for me keeping your jacket so long."

"I don't want those! Jeez, Nikki. Okay. Come inside. It's too hot out here anyway. You can keep me company while I pack."

It was cool and musty in Lyla's room. Two brown pasteboard boxes filled with books sat on the extra bed next to the open blue suitcase. The built-in shelf where Lyla kept her makeup mirror and curling iron was bare. Her Lava Lamp was missing. The posters were gone from the walls, light-colored rectangles on the painted concrete showing where they'd been. Nikki felt weird to be here. The last conversation she'd had with her cousin was in this room. The last fight. They used to fight all the time as kids, because . . . well, sisters fight. But Lyla didn't seem like a sister now, she seemed like a distant stranger, and Nikki wasn't going to fight today anyway. She'd promised herself that. She watched Lyla pulling skirts and blouses off hangers, rolling them tightly and tucking them inside the suitcase. "When are you leaving?" she asked.

"Tomorrow afternoon. I've got one more final."

"Man. You pack early."

Lyla gave her a look.

"Sorry. I didn't mean anything by it. So, what kind of job in Illinois?"

"Indiana. It's a Special Olympics camp."

"Oh. You'll like that, right?"

"Hope so."

Lyla was a Special Ed major; she planned to teach special needs kids in elementary school—something Nikki never really got. Why would a person want to do that all day? She watched Lyla fold the jean jacket, lay it on top of one of the book boxes. Her cousin turned to the built-in chest and started pulling T-shirts and dungarees out of the drawers. "How about you?" Lyla said over her shoulder.

"Hunh?"

"What kind of job are you working?"

Nikki's hesitation betrayed the lie before she answered. "Oh, I've been painting houses with friends."

Lyla glanced back at her—a look that said, *I don't believe you*—but aloud, she asked, "Good money?"

"It's all right." Nikki grabbed a T-shirt, rolled it into a tight bundle, and laid it in the suitcase. "So, they don't let you keep your same room over the summer? I could stay here, and, like, you know, hold it till you get back."

"They don't do that. Anyway, I'm not coming back. I'm transferring to OU next fall."

"Yeah?" Nikki felt herself reeling, a gravityless freefall, as if the earth were spinning away from her. She sat down on the bed. "That's like in another town, right?"

"It's in—hey. Are you all right?" Lyla was standing over her, frowning. Nikki shook her head.

"I'm good. I'm just . . . hungry, I think."

Lyla went immediately to a book box and dug out a jar of Peter Pan and a sleeve of saltines. She made Nikki a half dozen peanut butter crackers, left for a few minutes and came back with a bottle of Coke. But see, man, that was it, Nikki realized as she scarfed down the crackers, sipped the cold Coke: she did feel better. The sugar and caffeine helped. The protein helped. Being inside where it was cool helped. But it was Lyla, really. Lyla: her ticket to safety, the one who was straight enough to take care of her, the one who had always tethered her to . . . family. Not the whole family. Not Nikki's straight uptight aunt and uncle and weird cousins and self-centered needy mother, but to the two who had always loved her unconditionally and treated her like she was worth something: Nana and Grandpa. And now Lyla wouldn't be nearby, not even across campus for Nikki to ignore, turn her face away from, act like she didn't see. Lyla sat down next to her on the bed. "When's the last time you ate?" she said.

"I don't know. Like, yesterday, I guess."

"Are you pregnant?"

"What? No! God no."

"Well, that's good. Come back with me to Bartlesville. My dad can help you get a job."

"I've *got* a job!"

"Right."

Nikki made to stand up, but Lyla touched her hand. "Okay, not Bartlesville. I get that. I'll take you to Cedar. Nana and Grandpa would love to see you. They'd be happy for you to stay there till you . . . get it together."

"I've got it together."

Lyla snorted. Nikki was silent. She felt Lyla's arm across her shoulder. Her cousin tried to draw her into a hug, but Nikki remained stiff, unyielding. If she yielded even a quarter inch, she would dissolve into shakes and sobs and shudders. Lyla withdrew her arm. "Listen. It doesn't have to be like this," she said. "You could get your GED, go to college."

"And do what?"

"Whatever you want."

"Can I borrow twenty bucks?" Nikki said. "Just till I get paid."

"How is that going to help anything? You'll just blow it on drugs or something."

Nikki would have stormed out right then, but she'd promised herself she wouldn't fight. She'd promised herself to get some money and give it to Floyd so he would . . . she didn't know what . . . forgive her. Share good times with her again. She said quietly, looking down at her hands, "I need it for rent, Lyla. I'll pay you back. Honest. I'll mail it to you in Bartlesville. Or Indiana or whatever." She looked up. "Please?"

Lyla went to her purse on the bureau and took a twenty out of her billfold. She sat down beside Nikki again but didn't hold out the bill. "You can get grant money to go to college. I'll help you fill out the application." Nikki waited. "What are you ever going to do with yourself?" Lyla said. "Work fast food and clean toilets the rest of your life?"

"I'm going to be an artist! A photographer, maybe. I'm going to New York to study!"

"Where at?"

"How the hell do I know? They got art colleges, surely! It's fucking New York!"

"You don't have to be profane."

"Well, quit pushing me! Jesus."

"I'll help you," Lyla said. "We'll go to a library and look it up, where's the best place to study art photography. The most affordable," said Lyla the pragmatist. "But you're still going to need your GED."

"I don't even know what that is."

"It's like an alternative high school diploma. You study for it and take a test."

"Oh, yeah. I'm so great at that."

"You can do it, Nikki. You can do anything you want. Come to Cedar this summer while I'm at camp, stay with Nana and Grandpa, and when I get back, I'll take you with me. You can take art classes at OU. I'll help you get started."

"Why would you even do that?"

"You're my cousin. We're family." Lyla paused. "You can always come home, Nik," she said softly.

Nikki imagined it: the long, hot, sweaty summer in that tiny hick town, bored out of her skull and going nowhere but to church with her grandparents, no bars, no Floyd, no friends, nothing to tamp down the fire and hunger, just endless hot days of daytime TV and locust whine. She knew she would run after a week—and then her grandparents would be hurt worse than ever. Then they would know how worthless and hopeless she truly was.

"I'll think about it," she said.

The silence grew long. Nikki could smell the flowery shampoo in her cousin's hair. Clairol Herbal Essence. The scent was almost like the sweet sound of saxophone in the night, almost that yearning. She felt herself softening. Maybe Lyla felt it too, because she handed her the twenty. "Take that to your roommates," she said. "Be back here by two o'clock tomorrow. We'll drive down to Cedar. I'll call my mom and tell her I'll be home later. Okay? Nikki? Okay?"

Nikki wouldn't look her in the eye. "Okay." She stood up and stuffed the twenty in her pocket.

"Two o'clock. Don't be late, all right? You can help me load the car."

HER real intention was to take the money to Floyd. It really was. She didn't have to go by the bar—it wasn't even on the way. But the day was so hot and bright when she came out of Lyla's dorm, and she thought how good a cold beer would taste, and it was almost Happy Hour, she'd have enough money to drink one draft, okay, maybe two, and then she would buy Floyd some cigarettes at QuikTrip, and a pack for herself so she could quit mooching, and she'd still have enough money to give him toward her part of the rent.

A couple of hours later she stood in the restroom at Granny's examining her face in the mirror. She was getting old, she decided. Everything was getting old. The whole freaking world. Anyway, she was born old, right?

No. How she was born was selfish and stupid.

She was born a person who would do stupid crap on impulse, and then later find out it messed everything up. Like buying round after round of pitchers for a table of longhair hippie freaks and their girl-friends when she didn't even like them. They made her feel . . . judged. Like the freaks in Sonora. And now she only had five bucks left and some change; that wasn't going to fix anything. Why did she do crap like this? Lyla never did. All their lives her cousin had chided her: can't you for once in your life, Nikki, for God's sake, just *think?* But Nikki couldn't think. She didn't know why she did what she did, so how could she help it? Nobody but Floyd understood this. Not even him. Not anymore. A wave of emptiness slid over her. She left the

restroom, weaved her way toward the longhairs. She stood beside
their table and knocked back two beers while the room moved in
slow motion around her. No one was paying her any attention. She
poured a third beer, took it with her when she walked out the door.

It was still daylight out but sliding toward evening. Apricot-colored
light slanted between the brick buildings across the way, slid gold
along the concrete. The soft May air was like memory on her skin.
She couldn't go back to Floyd's apartment now. She just couldn't.
She turned south toward the redneck bar down the street, stood
on the sidewalk listening to the country-and-western music inside.
Her pulse thrummed. There were no windows, just a blank raggedy
wooden wall, a sign over the door: Ted's. For a moment, standing
in front of the bar with the sun slanting behind her and the music
thumping, the evening air kissing her skin, the beer swimming in her
blood—just enough, just that light perfect buzz—Nikki felt it like
that Joan Baez song. Like she could have died then and there. She
drained her beer, set the glass on the sidewalk. When she pushed
through the door, the sound and smell swelled.

The place was six o'clock lively—not wild yet, but that good kind
of anticipation-lively, because the beer hadn't turned mean yet and
nobody remembered yesterday and the whole night was still ahead.
She climbed onto a barstool and ordered a draw, told the bartender
to run a tab. "We don't do tabs here," he said. The five was stuffed
deep in her pocket. She had promised herself she was not going to
spend it. She turned to look at the room. From the pool tables in the
back came a constant syncopated *crack!* and then *crack!* as the balls
smacked each other. Along the wall opposite was a row of wooden
booths. A Native couple sat together on one side of a booth. The
pitcher on the table in front of them was half full. "Okay. Just give
me a glass of water," she said. "I see my friends there." She took her
water, went to their booth and slid in.

"Y'all mind? I'm waiting for somebody and those yahoos at the bar won't leave me alone." Nikki nodded at two rednecks in ball caps nursing beers at the far end. The couple looked surprised. Or not surprised so much as baffled, like, is this white chick lost? But they nodded. She finished her water, reached for their pitcher. Nikki had figured she'd know them from one of the parties at the apartment, but she didn't. She got their names, Eddie and Joquita, told them her name was Nyla, but then immediately forgot she'd told them, so the whole rest of the night, if somebody called her Nyla, she wouldn't react till they'd said it like five times. And there was a whole rest of the night. A long night. A bad one.

She remembered some moments; others were brownouts. Not total blackouts, at first, because images stayed with her, and smells. The pool balls going *crack! rollrumblemumble* and the cue sticks pointed up to the ceiling at the back of the bar, dancing and dipping, the smell of beer sweet and sour in her nostrils, and the tabletop sticky beneath her elbows; the ashtray spilling out twisted, smashed butts and the round wet circles where the beer glasses sweated and Willie Nelson on the jukebox singing about blue eyes crying in the rain, over and over. She remembered standing on the street in front of the bar, the streetlight spinning, remembered stumbling to the curb to throw up. Then she'd felt better. Then she was at a party, everybody singing, beer bottles rolling around on a green linoleum floor. Then she was walking somewhere, a dark street, and she threw up on somebody's lawn. Then she thought she could drink some more. Then she lost hours.

She came out of a blackout sprawled across the seat of a truck with a guy's hands running over her, up the legs of her cutoffs, inside her shirt. He wasn't Indian. Not a redneck. Not a longhair. Just some dude with Vitalis hair. He reeked of whiskey. She tried to push his hands away, but they were like the roaches on the burgundy couch in L.A., his fingers running everywhere, everywhere, she couldn't brush them away. She tried to say *stop it*, but her mouth wouldn't work. It was dark inside the truck, and also outside. They were . . . where? Out in the country? No, she could see a brick building beside the open window. Brick buildings on both sides. They were in an alley somewhere. A black blind alley. Not a new life. Not a new person. Just the same old, same old Nikki, the same sickness and loathing. She thought she could just surrender, just pass out again, then she wouldn't know anything. Wouldn't have to remember. *You can do anything, Nikki.* Her cousin's voice. And Floyd's: *Be whatever you want, girl.* "I got . . . to pee," she said, her tongue thick. "Let me up, man. I got to pee."

The dude mumbled against her shoulder. He was trying to push her shorts down, but he was so drunk he could only fumble. "Get off me," Nikki said, louder. "I'm going to puke all over your sorry ass." She'd found her voice now, strong, even if the words were slurred. The guy tried to sit up, but the gear shift was in the way. Nikki shoved him over, wiggled out from underneath, slid to the far door. "I'll be right back," she said.

She started walking. She knew where east was. Out toward the river. Out past Braum's and Pizza Hut and the Oak Park Motel and all the other places she was never going to work. The sky was getting lighter. She was barefoot—she'd lost her sandals somewhere. Lost her five dollars too—her pockets were empty. And she was thirsty as hell. But daylight was coming, a grayish lifting to the air, and then it was a little lighter, and a little lighter, as she walked toward the river bridge. She had a new song inside her, not the same rhythm as *I won't be her anymore, I'll be a new me*, because she would always be her. She would always be Nikki. But she could do anything. Be anything. She was heading east, toward New York, and dawn was breaking over the river, great long sweeps of pink and orange and fuchsia, and the sky above a wash of turquoise; the sun would be up soon, she told herself, and then, in the next breath, the next acute, aching inkling, there it was, lifting over the horizon: perfect fire and glory. Beautiful enough to blind her.

That Grief, That Fury

My son Floyd was one the other kids picked on. I also have two daughters. Had. Have. Delores and Nemo. Nobody picked on the girls though, that I ever saw. They just grew up. Delores got cancer in her ovaries and died. Nemo moved to Tucson. My son Floyd, he's dead too. Him and some other boys went off the side of a mountain in a car over by Tahlequah. But that's not what I think about. I think about how the other kids picked on him when he was little.

We lived in West Tulsa then. Well, I still do, but we lived in a different house then. Over on Quanah. I'd quit whatever I was doing and go out to the porch when I heard them, this mess of kids' voices hollering and laughing, coming home from school. I'd see Floyd walking in the still center of them. The other kids would be swarming around him, yelling, making faces.

Teasing him. They didn't fight him much because he'd fight back—he'd turn wild if they tried to touch him—but they could say anything in the world to him they wanted, he'd just turn his face to the ground and go on. I don't even know what all it was about. It wasn't just about him being Indian because there were other Indian families around and those kids never got it bad like Floyd did. The white kids just wouldn't leave him alone. They'd do things like put a sign on his back, DEBBIE ARNOLD LOVES FLOYD SIXKILLER, and then wait till that girl seen it and she'd cry and act like she was going to die and run tell the teacher. Then the kids would follow Floyd all the way home from school shouting it. Just shaming him. I told

95

him to fight them. I said, don't wait till they hit you first, you light into them when they start teasing you like that. But he wouldn't do it. Not when it was only just words.

Floyd moved like . . . I don't know, like one of these underwater creatures or something, all jerky-like and delicate. If some of them tried to hit him, he'd change, become a thing whirling, twisting, like a twister, a dust devil, arms and legs flying. They couldn't touch him then. They were scared of him like that. But they could say shit to him, and he'd just float his hands in the air and duck his head. My heart hurt so bad, watching him. I guess that's the reason it stays in my mind so much.

He went over towards Tahlequah quick as he could once he got grown, went to school there at the college. He never came home much. He'd call Delores once in a while and ask us to come see him, but I wouldn't go. I'd left that town twenty years ago, and I didn't care to go back. But one morning, after he was living there about a year, Delores come to the house and told me she was going. She stood in the kitchen door the longest time, holding the car keys in her hand. Big in the doorway, letting cold air in. Looking at me. Finally I said, all right, let me get my purse, and we drove to Tahlequah to see Floyd.

I started feeling sick the minute we come over the top of the hill west of town. It was winter. I looked down at the tops of the buildings on Muskogee cutting sideways below us and the stark trees of the park rising up on the other side, and I just got sick. We turned north towards the college, and I didn't say anything. I had to sit real still. Every house was just the same—same color, same place on the street, same everything. Delores asked me what was the matter, but I just sat with my mouth shut and looked at the windshield.

She stopped at the QuikTrip by Goingsnake and went in for some pop and a pack of cigarettes. I sat in the car. I thought my chest would just collapse. That's the street we lived on when I was in high school. Whatever I'd kept from thinking about all those years rose up then, and I couldn't see or feel or think nothing but what it felt like to leave the house in the mornings and walk to school. Just nothing but sickness and anger and shame.

I used to ask myself if things would've been different if I'd went to some other family someplace else besides Tahlequah—not even anywhere around Cherokee County, I mean. Like a place where there's no Indians at all. Or not so much if things would've been different but if I would have been. Or felt different. Or acted different anyway. It wasn't like they did me the way those kids in Tulsa done Floyd. It was something more weaving in and out, more invisible in the air. But you could feel it every minute. Contempt, I guess. Or else like *I* was invisible. I'd give some white woman my money at the Safeway, she'd give the change back like she was giving it to the ether. Like she could look right through my skin to the chewing gum rack behind me.

I sat in the car and watched Delores through the plate-glass window. I watched her pay for her pop and pick up the paper sack. The boy handed back her change, and I watched her turn and move heavy through the cardboard cutouts and stacks of six-packs on special. She pushed on the glass door. I couldn't tell if she felt it like I felt it. Like that white boy sold a soda pop, sacked it, handed back some dimes and quarters to a person invisible, an old unfortunate memory of a thing, taking up the same space on the planet.

Delores looked at me funny when she got back in the car. "You sick or something?" she said.

I *was* sick, though I didn't want to tell it. Sick to be back in Tahlequah—and something else too, some kind of hurtful squeezed-up longing I couldn't understand or name. I shook my head, and she started the car. In a minute we pulled up in front of some squat red-brick apartments that was part of the college and got out of the car and went in to see Floyd.

He was living with Indians then. All tribes, all mixed, not just Cherokee—Otoe and Pawnee and Yuchi and Creek and I don't even remember now, there was so many of them living in that apartment and the ones next to it. Lots of Indians went to that school then. Still do, I guess. And Floyd was doing good. He was better than I ever saw him. He was still quiet, hardly said anything, but he stood leaning against the wall in the kitchen, watching everything, and he looked good. Looked peaceful. Proud.

We had us a little party then, drank some beers because I think it was somebody's birthday, and about halfway through the night I got up and went outside. I'd nearly forgot I was in Tahlequah because we were having a good time. I stood in the yard in front of those red-brick apartments and looked straight up at the stars pricking lights in the sky with no moon. I looked south as far as I could see, which wasn't far because the buildings of the college stood in the way, and I thought to myself it was just strange. I'd left this town because I couldn't ever feel like I belonged here. And it turned out to be the one place my son Floyd found where he did belong.

I heard Delores come out the door behind me. "Mama? What's wrong?"

I didn't answer. The question was too big. Everything was wrong. From day one. From even before I could remember, to the first day of my own mama, whoever she was. They won't let you find out. There's laws against it. I told Delores I just needed some air.

"It's cold out here," she said.

"I guess."

"You want me to get your coat?"

"No. Go on. I'll be in in a minute."

I could feel her shivering in her shirtsleeves. "Maybe we ought to start home," she said.

I shook my head. "You like this place?" I asked her.

"It's all right. Plumbing works good, hey?" And she laughed. We both laughed. That was the biggest trouble we had at that house on Quanah. Landlord wouldn't fix nothing. I knew she thought I meant did she like the apartment where Floyd was living, but that wasn't what I meant. I just let it go. I could hear them singing inside the house then—somebody'd opened the window to let some of the smoke out, I guess—and the sound gave me that old squeezed-up feeling, but it didn't hurt now. It felt good. So we went back in.

We stayed the whole night. Me and Delores went to sleep in the bedroom while they were still singing in the front room. When we woke up, Floyd was asleep on the floor. He took us out to breakfast, to that good cafe downtown, fried eggs and sausage and biscuits and gravy. "You can't afford this," I told him. "How can you afford this?"

"I got a job now. I'm working maintenance at the college—didn't Delores tell you?"

"No."

Delores said, "Well, I did, Mama. You just forgot."

But I didn't forget. I wouldn't forget that. I watched Floyd walk up to the register. I could hear the forks and plates clattering all around me, people talking. The sun was shining in through the front windows and the room smelled like coffee and frying bacon, and everybody in it was white but me and my son and daughter, but nobody was looking at us. Floyd's hair was grown out now, almost down to his shoulders, all black and sleek and shiny, and his hands were slim and long, and when he pulled some bills out of his pocket and handed them to the lady, it was like . . . I don't know how to explain it. Like his hands were saying something I couldn't understand. Like they were making a sign that said something silent in the air. He must have felt me watching, because he turned and looked at me. He didn't smile or nothing, but his look said, see, Mama? I'm doing good now. Quit your worrying. And he was. I knew he was, then.

In the car on the way home Delores kept asking me what was the matter, and I kept saying, nothing, it's nothing, till finally she quit asking. Her radio was broke so we just listened to her old car's loud motor the whole rest of the drive to West Tulsa. When we pulled up in front of the house, I said, "Mr. Spellman used to work in maintenance at the college. That's all." At first she looked at me like she didn't know what I was talking about, then she took in a breath, like, oh, okay. She started to say something else, but I reached for the door handle and got out.

AFTER that first trip to Tahlequah, seemed like I couldn't stop. It was like an old wound had got broke open and started bleeding, and I couldn't make it scab over again the way I could when I was young. I couldn't drink it healed—I'd quit trying that a long time ago. Drinking only ever lets you forget for a little while anyway. I tried going to that Spanish church over on Nogales, I thought maybe that would be different enough, but it wasn't, because church, well, no matter how much the Spellmans made me go, I never did feel right there. Not that I felt right anywhere.

They weren't bad people, the Spellmans. They didn't mean to be. That's part of what makes it hard. If you could just hate them, maybe it would've been easier. I mean hate them only. Without anything else mixed in. They were old already when they got me, and I think that made it hard too. They didn't know how to be with a child. Mr. Spellman worked maintenance at the college, that's how he always said it, but really he was just a custodian. He swept and mopped the floors in the classrooms, emptied the trash, fixed the boilers sometimes. Mrs. Spellman stayed home with me. They thought they were giving me a good life, thought they were saving me from being a heathen. They didn't say that out loud, but I knew that's what they thought.

You know, you shut the door on something, you think that's going to be the end of it, it won't bother you anymore. I moved to Tulsa. I had my kids, my job at Bama Pies, a good enough place to live. The Spellmans died a long time ago, I didn't have to go back to that place ever again. But then we took that trip to see Floyd, and something changed in me. Old memories started coming in my mind, day and night, awake or sleeping, whether I was washing dishes or playing bingo or walking to the store. I'd all of a sudden remember hiding under the honeysuckle vines along the fence in the backyard, and I'd feel the cold air, my breath like a white cloud under the vines, how I'd dream my mother was going to ride up in the yard on a painted pony with a white feather in her hair and pull me up behind her and take me home, because I was still so little then, I didn't have any way to picture Indians except like how they looked on TV—wild yelling men on horses riding in circles around wagons or the beautiful Indian princess named Morning Star—and I'd have to choose Morning Star. I told myself that's who my mother was. Or I'd remember the clang and echo in the halls at the junior high school, the scratched gray steel on the front of my locker, my blue math book all scuffed and smelling like mildew, the damp weight of it under my arm, the taste of cigarettes in my mouth like an old ashtray from where I'd been smoking out back of the gym. I'd remember sitting on a swing at the park when I was really little, before I even started school, how I'd be watching the clear waters in the town branch rippling over the stones, and I'd hear voices there, singing in the water. But if I got off the swing and went near, the singing stopped. I remembered one time coming out of the Safeway eating a Three Musketeers bar, the white nougat showing my teeth marks under the brown chocolate, and when I looked up, she was coming in the door on her way to grocery shop, and I tried to hide the bar behind my back, but she'd already seen me; she dragged me to the car and took me home and whipped me, and I kept shouting, I didn't steal it! I didn't steal it!, and she kept whipping me until I told her where I got the money, and then she whipped me some more, not for stealing the candy but for stealing the nickel I was supposed to give to my troop leader for my Brownie dues.

I don't want to make it sound like they hit me all the time. They didn't. Mr. Spellman never laid a hand on me, and Mrs. Spellman with her flyswatter was about like a bee sting, except that time over the Brownie money, and I think that was because she was scared. I think she felt like she had to beat the thief out of me, beat the Indian out of me, because if she didn't do it then, when I was eight years old, it would only get worse. The whippings, though, they're what you remember. And that feeling like you don't belong.

I had other memories, too, but Mrs. Spellman said they couldn't be memories because she said they got me when I was a baby, too little to remember. She showed me the papers. Not all of the papers, just the page that said Baby Girl Spellman and gave their names for my mother and father and the date they adopted me, a few days after my birthday—or the date they said was my birthday. October 7, 1940. But in my heart, I knew that wasn't true. I knew I had memories from before I went to live there—some kind of feeling, a smell or something, a room. I lost them, though. Those memories. I don't know when. Sometime when I was pretty young because I remember sitting at my desk in second grade trying to call them up, but it would be like a moth fluttering in the back of my mind. Except not a white moth, a dark one. Like a moth shadow, batting, batting against the screen.

I started thinking about it again, what I used to think about every day of my life when I was a kid, and then what I tried to not think about for years, because it was useless, just a useless, hopeless circle, you couldn't get anywhere. But after we went to see Floyd that time I couldn't stop thinking about it: how to find my family. My mother.

How to find out what tribe she was. What tribe *I* was. I'd tried once, after I moved to Tulsa, but they seal all the records. They don't want you to know nothing, not her name or where she lived. Who her people were. Like she wasn't real, whoever it was that gave birth to you. Like she was just a ghost person who couldn't really exist. I didn't know how to break through.

I'd sit at the kitchen table in my little house on Quanah and try to make those first good memories come back, but I couldn't get even the moth flutters anymore. I couldn't get anything but the hard memories from Tahlequah. I started thinking, what if Mrs. Spellman was telling the truth? What if they *did* get me when I was just born? What if my birthday is my real birthday? I didn't have the paper she showed me, just an amended birth certificate I'd written away for when I needed to get my Social Security card. It had their names for my parents and the name they gave me, Juanita Ruth Spellman, and the same birth date. It said I was born in Tulsa County, but it didn't say where. That could mean anything. Mrs. Spellman died years ago, and then Mr. Spellman, too, right after. There was nobody to ask. Even if they would've told.

When Mr. Spellman died, his niece in Arkansas wrote me a letter. I didn't know how she had my address, I barely remembered her. I'd only ever seen her once or twice. She said the Spellmans had left some things for me. They were in a storage unit in Tahlequah, she said, because she'd had to sell the house. She taped the key to the page with Scotch tape and drew directions for a storage place on Downing Street. But I threw the letter away. I never even peeled off the key. I'd shut that door already—that's how I felt. I was with Nemo's daddy then, he was jealous about everything, and anyway, we didn't have a car.

But sitting at my kitchen table that winter, I started thinking, well, what if there was something in there? What if my real birth certificate was there? The true one. With my mother's name. Or some pictures from when I was little. Or my adoption papers with that page Mrs. Spellman showed me. Just anything that could tell me how to start. I knew I could find that storage place, no problem, and maybe the people that ran it would have my name, or the name the niece would have put it under, Juanita Spellman, even if I didn't have the key. I didn't want to ask Delores to take me to Tahlequah. I didn't want to talk about it. I never told my kids nothing. They knew I was adopted, and they knew the people that adopted me were dead, but that's all. If they ever asked, I'd just say I grew up with a white family in Tahlequah, there was nothing else to tell. I think they knew it went deeper than that—or Floyd and Delores did—but they never pushed.

I made up my mind to go. I started saving money for the bus ticket. I quit buying cookies, quit going to bingo. I'd walk along Southwest Boulevard and pick up pop cans, but it takes a lot of pop cans to add up to enough weight to get any kind of money. By the time I had enough saved, the weather was turning warm.

Early one morning I rode a city bus to the downtown station and got on a Greyhound to Muskogee, and then I had to wait three hours in Muskogee for the next bus to Tahlequah, so it was afternoon when I stepped down by the square next to the courthouse. I wouldn't let the old feelings slide over me, I just set out walking straight over to Downing Street. I climbed the hill, walking pretty fast, heading east. I had a pushing feeling in me, like I was late for something, even though that made no sense. I'd already waited all these years. I walked and I walked, all the way out past the new city hospital, and I didn't see any storage units or anything that looked even close. When I got to the edge of town, where they'd built those big new wide roads, I turned around and walked back. I went inside a few businesses, a pizza place and an ice cream store, but it was just kids working there. They didn't know anything about any storage businesses on Downing Street or anyplace else. I stopped in at the Oak Park Motel, and the man behind the desk said, yes, he'd been there several years, and no, there wasn't any storage businesses on Downing Street, at least not since 1968 when he bought the motel. I walked back out, around past the swimming pool, to the street.

I didn't know what to do next. It was like a whole new grief. I could have kicked myself for putting so much store in it. For thinking there might be some kind of answer, or that they would really leave me anything, or that anybody would treat me straight up and not trick me like that niece of Mr. Spellman's tricked me for no reason I could think of except meanness. Just to make me feel like a fool. I had that heartsickness, that grief, and also the old fury. Then it was like I wasn't even making the decision, I just set out walking. I crossed Downing Street, cut north through a side street and then there I was. On Goingsnake Street.

My heart wound up tighter and tighter the closer I got. My feet were carrying me of their own strength, and when I reached the yard, I stopped. I felt like every drop of blood drained out of me. I was ready for the house to look smaller than I remembered, or shabbier, or nastier, or some other kind of way. I wasn't ready for it to be a brick ranch house with a garage and white trim. The niece must've sold the lot a long time ago, because the house wasn't even that new. The paint around the windows was starting to flake. I felt like, well, what did you expect? Some words jumped in my mind then, saying the same thing over and over: *wipe the slate clean, wipe the slate clean.* That's what they did, what they'd always done. Wiped the slate clean. No past, no true papers, not even an ugly little gray-shingled frame house with a carport and a backyard with honeysuckle vines covering the fence. Nothing to show I once lived there, or didn't live there, or came from any real place at all.

I kept going along Goingsnake. When I reached the corner at
Muskogee, I didn't turn left towards the bus stop but right towards
the college. I didn't care if I was sweating and my skirt was sticking
to my legs and I had blisters between my toes from walking all day
in rubber thongs. I didn't even care when the white kids looked at
me funny while I was walking past the student union. I just kept on
towards the redbrick apartments where my son lived. I knocked at
the door, and nobody answered for the longest, and then finally a
big, sleepy-looking Indian kid come to the door. I remembered him
from the party. He said Floyd moved out months ago.

"Do you know where he's living?" I said.

The boy shrugged. "I think some apartments over on Keetoowah.
I'm not sure."

I turned, the raw places between my toes burning fire now. I went
to the end of the row of apartments and turned north and kept walking, right up to the front door of W.W. Hastings Indian Hospital.
Because that's all I had—not the paper Mrs. Spellman showed me
but the memory burned in my mind of what it said: Name of Child:
Baby Girl Spellman. Date of Birth: *10/7/40* Race or Color: *I*

Race or Color: I

The one place I know of for sure where Indian babies get born is
Indian hospitals. There's an Indian hospital in Claremore, but that's
not Tulsa County. Talihina's got one, but that's even farther away. I
thought, maybe it wasn't even Tulsa County. Maybe that was just
one more of their lies. If there's someplace that would tell you the
truth, I thought, this ought to be it.

I walked in through the glass doors. I'd expected it would be all
Indians working there, but the lady behind the desk was a white lady,
or anyhow she looked it. Her hair was tinted bluish gray, poofed up
and ratted. She said, "Can I help you, dear?"

"How much does it cost to get a copy of some records? A birth certificate. For somebody born in 1940?"

The smile she gave me withered my whole insides. She didn't intend for it to be a mean smile—she meant it to be kind. That's what made it bad. The sound in her voice when she answered matched her smile. "We don't keep those records here, dear," she said, and the sound told me I was the stupidest person in the world. "You'll have to write to the Department of Health Division of Vital Records in Oklahoma City for that."

I looked at her a minute. "I already did that," I said. I could sense her watching me while I went back out the door. I stood on the front walk. My head was dizzy. I felt like I might fall down. A Cherokee family was getting out of their car in the parking lot, an old man and a woman and four little kids. They came towards me, and an Indian guy with his hair tied back was coming up the sidewalk from the other side, and I had a rage in me like I hadn't felt since my worst bad drinking days. It could have swept across like a great wind and knocked out those Indians walking towards me knowing their tribe and where they came from and how to walk inside those glass doors and give the lady their card that proved it, and it could have knocked out the lady herself, with her ratted hair and her kind, contemptuous smile. It could have knocked out all the buildings in front of me—those apartments where Floyd used to live with Indian boys and the brick buildings of the college and all the buildings in the town where Cherokee words are written on the street signs and stenciled out across the windows of the bank. My rage could have swept all the way west to Tulsa, and beyond Tulsa, to the earth's end. It could have knocked out the whole world.

I was trembling. My feet were burning. I looked down and saw my bare feet flat on the hot concrete. I didn't even know I'd stepped out of my shoes. I left those cheap black rubber thongs there, a space apart, pointing south, like the person wearing them had just vanished. I started walking towards the Greyhound bus stop downtown.

I LIMPED from the curb to Delores's car, and when I got in with no shoes, just my purse tight in my hand, I could tell Delores was scared. But she didn't say anything, and I didn't. When we got to my house, she parked and came in, made me lay down on the sofa with my feet up while she washed them and dabbed on the Bactine and wrapped them in cotton strips she tore from a clean dish towel. She sat in the chair and looked at me. She wouldn't ask, but she wasn't leaving till I told her—if not everything, at least something. Where I'd been. What I was doing at the Tulsa Greyhound station at ten o'clock at night with no shoes. I asked her to turn on the TV, but she didn't. I could feel the power of her waiting, and for a minute it was like she was me, waiting all my life to hear the truth, and I could feel then how bad it was, me not telling my kids anything, but I could feel the clot in my throat, too, like it had been since I could remember, like somebody jammed cotton wadding deep inside there, like even if I had a hundred mouths, a hundred tongues, I would never be able to speak. I asked her did she have any aspirin in her purse. She got up and went to the kitchen and came back with a glass of water and a little tin box of Anacin and gave me two.

I swallowed the tablets. "How come you didn't tell me Floyd moved?" I said.

"Floyd moved? Where to?" She stood over me, frowning. "How'd you know that?"

"I went to see him, but they said he don't live there anymore."

"Why didn't you tell me you were going? You know I would've drove you." When I didn't say anything, she got up and went to the kitchen. I could hear her slamming things in there, running water in the sink, washing dishes. I heard her put on a pot of coffee. She didn't come back till it quit perking. She brought a cup for her and one for me. She lit a cigarette, sat kind of hunched toward the coffee table. Delores had her daddy's same smooth flat features, his pretty mouth and high forehead. But she looked troubled in a way Joe never did.

I said, "You remember when we lived with your daddy's folks in Tahlequah?"

Her head flew up like a shot. She stared at me. "No. When?"

"You were little."

"How come you never told me that?" She was all reared up alert, like a deer set to run. "Why don't we ever see them? Let's go see them."

"Government moved them to California."

"When?"

"Long time ago."

"How come you never said anything about that? Mama? How come you never say anything about anything!"

And I couldn't answer. I don't know who jammed that wadding down my throat. Or why. Or when. She was staring at me so hard, I wanted to give her something. I said, "I met him at a party."

"Who? My daddy?"

I nodded. The wadding felt tight and dry in my mouth. I drank some coffee. "He'd just got home from the service and he had on his army uniform. He walked in the kitchen with a beer in his hand, his hair slicked back, them gold buttons shining. I thought he was the best-looking thing I'd ever seen in my life."

She waited for me to say something more and when I didn't she said, real soft, like she didn't want to spook me, "Where was that?"

"The party? Somebody's uncle's place. I don't remember. I'd snuck out of the house to go."

She waited again. Finally said, "How old were you?"

"Sixteen."

"How old was my daddy?"

"I don't remember." She waited some more. Kept looking at me. "Twenty-one."

And then, because she kept waiting, looking at me and waiting, and because those early days with Joe was one thing I felt like I could talk about, then, a little, and because every time I hushed, Delores would nudge me with a question like *when was that?* or *where'd you go then?*, holding her breath, listening hard to every answer, and because I wanted to make up for all my years of not saying anything, I told her about how me and Joe met at that party, him looking at me and me looking at him all night while the party went on around us, until it got near dawn and gray light started coming in through the curtains. I jumped up, shouting about I had to go, this minute! I was going to get creamed if my parents found out I wasn't in my bed! Joe stood up and got the keys to his brother's truck and drove me home and waited while I snuck in my bedroom window, but they didn't catch me, and I didn't get creamed, and I'd already made a date to meet Joe next night on the corner after my parents went to bed. I told her how me and him lived with his brother's family after I got kicked out of the house, then moved in with his parents when we found out I was pregnant. I told her how her daddy talked in stories. He wouldn't ever tell you what he was thinking or his opinions on anything, but if you asked him a question, he'd answer with a story. Or sometimes even if you didn't ask. I told her I was crazy about him. Just crazy head-over-heels in love with Joe Sixkiller from the minute I laid eyes on him.

"For real?" she said, and the sadness in her face said all the things she couldn't say out loud, like why the hell did you leave him then? Why did you spend all them bad years with that sonofabitching Larry? And why would you let my daddy go away from us all and get killed?

"For real," I answered. But then I didn't want to talk anymore. Or I couldn't. I laid back down on the sofa and shut my eyes. I started breathing slow, slow, so she would think I was sleeping. I finally heard her go out and start the car.

I LIED to Delores. I didn't mean to—I just didn't want her thinking anything bad about her daddy. I wasn't sixteen when I met him. I was fourteen. And Joe wasn't twenty-one, he was twenty-four. Ten years older. Where that sixteen come from is that's how old I was when Delores was born. She probably could have figured that out if she wanted. I wasn't lying when I said he was the best-looking man I'd ever seen in my life. That's the truth. But I had a hard time about him being Indian. Oh, I can't explain that. I wish I could. It was 1954, there was lots of prejudice against Indians then. You'd think the Cherokee capital would be one place you wouldn't see it, but, really, I think that just made it worse. I wasn't part of them anyway—I wasn't Cherokee, didn't grow up Indian, didn't have a clan, a history. I didn't even look like them. Not really. And for sure I wasn't part of the white kids. Then I met Joe and I felt for a little while like I knew where I belonged. But I was still sneaking around. Not just from the Spellmans but also the kids at school—and what did they care? They never even seen me. I was a ghost person in the halls. The teachers didn't call on me, hardly ever. I was invisible to their eyes. I hated sitting there. I'd cut class, walk down through town, sit in the park for hours. My next report card, I got a whipping because I'd flunked all my classes, but I didn't care. I was sneaking out most nights anyway, to meet Joe.

That was probably the time I was the most mixed up in my life. It was like there was three of me. The ghost girl at school, walking with her head down. I wouldn't look anybody in the face, but I always felt like people were looking at me. Except I was invisible. All right, that's crazy, but that's how it felt. There was the me at home, talking back to my mother, sassing her—Mrs. Spellman, I mean. Any damn thing she told me to do, I wouldn't do it. I'd curse right at her sometimes. I had two faces at home, pouty and sullen, or defiant and spitting, but it was still the same Juanita either way—miserable and mean. Oh, I got along with my dad okay, because he never did anything but shake his head and lift his shoulders when I snapped at him. But Mrs. Spellman wouldn't give up. She kept trying to turn me into the daughter she wanted. Make your bed, Juanita. Come to the table now. Do your homework. Clear the table. Wash the dishes. Curl that stringy hair.

And then there was the me that rode in the truck at night with Joe, out to the river to party with his friends, or to just sit there alone in his brother's pickup and park. He couldn't get enough of me, and that made me feel good. He always had a case of beer and a pack of Winstons. We'd smoke and drink and neck, or if it was a party, we'd roam around the fire somebody always built on the gravel bar. We'd sing the songs, or he'd joke and laugh with the others, and Joe would keep a hand on me the whole time, just gentle on the top of my head or the small of my back, claiming me like that, but in a good way. Not like he owned me but like I belonged there beside him. That's what I'm saying. When I was with him, I belonged someplace. Or I belonged to somebody. But even then, unless I was really drunk, it was like there was the Indian on the outside—Wanita, the girl that belonged with Joe Sixkiller—but there was a different me inside. The fake girl. When Joe told somebody my name, I'd spell it out for them, W-A-N-I-T-A, because I thought that sounded more Indian. I still spell my name that way, and my last name is Cummings, from marrying Nemo's daddy. But that don't mean Juanita Spellman is dead. Except, really, she is.

All right. I can't explain that either.

NEXT time we went to see Floyd, things were different. It was more than three years after that first visit, and it was summer, and Floyd was a principal dancer at the Trail of Tears Outdoor Drama at Tsa-La-Gi. He wanted us to come see him. I didn't want to go because I knew all about Tsa-La-Gi, but him and Delores talked me into it. You see how it was. Those people made an outdoor drama, made a *pageant*, out of our dying and death. This show was run by white people. For white people to go see. So the white people who ran it could make money. I knew just what it was going to be.

Me and Delores come down the concrete steps just at dusk. The stage was way down steep below and the place for the people to sit was arranged in chairs in a big half circle up and down the wide cement steps, and there was a little makeshift mountain with ivy on it rising up in back of the stage. It wasn't dark yet when they started performing. And just like anybody could figure, there wasn't one Indian on that stage saying a word. There were a few real Indians down there—you could tell even from the top because they used their own hair, not big black braided wigs, and their skins were brown, not dyed that strange, awful red color like the dirt around Stillwater—but not a one of them had speaking parts. They shuffled across the stage in ragged blankets and stood around while the white people with red faces did all the acting. Those white people ranted and raved in great oratory voices like you never heard no Indian ever talk in your life, and besides which they were all men but for one woman who acted like a shivery piece of something with no better strength or brains than a chicken liver, and she was supposed to be a Cherokee woman. Well, I didn't even let myself get mad. I knew what it was going to be.

But then the dancing started, and something happened, and I just had to stop and wait. Because what I was doing was watching Floyd. He moved . . . I believe he moved more beautiful than any creature on this earth.

After that I just quit watching everything and waited for Floyd.

He danced every one of the dances. I believe every person sitting out there watching was watching for him. I believe they were all waiting for Floyd, every minute, just like me. When the music come on, everybody quickened. You could feel it all around, breath and heartbeat going quicker, and Delores sat up and leaned forward in her chair.

Floyd moved in the lights and the sound like he was soaring, sometimes twisting, sometimes prancing, and his hands that used to jerk or float like dead crappie reached up long and straight to the night sky so you half expected him to touch it, and he leaped in the air, leaped high, his feet small and weightless, like deer running, and the muscles snapped and jumped in his legs, his hair danced black shining, fluttering, flapping around him, and the lights swirled and turned colors, yellow and turquoise and lavender and pink, and my son moved like something born of spirit. Hardly covered in flesh. Hardly brushing the earth.

The play lasted long, and I didn't pay any attention to it. I sat through all the talking, waiting for the music, waiting for Floyd. It come near to the end finally, come to the last dance, and Floyd had to do battle with Death. They had this Death Dancer, all in black— black feathers, black mask. He'd been shaking his rattles all through the show, jumping up on the mountain in the spotlight, rattling his death rattles at those fake Cherokees, following them all the way from North Carolina and Georgia and all through the Civil War and beyond. And in the end, Floyd had to fight him.

The music rumbled and the lights moved and changed colors, and Floyd and Death fought all over that stage, up and down the make-shift mountain, all off to the side and in the middle, Floyd whirling and whirling like the dust devil he'd been, leaping in the amber and red and the smoke and the night air.

In the end—though I couldn't believe it, I never expected it, he was so strong and so beautiful—Death beat him. My son fell down dead in the middle of the stage. That Death Dancer shook his rattles high toward the sky, and the other dancers ran in a wild circle, flapping red and orange sheets like it was supposed to be fire, and Floyd lay still on his belly in the center of them with his hair spread out limp over his face on the ground.

I put my head down. I quit looking.

The white woman that was pretending to be Cherokee come over the loudspeaker and said Floyd wasn't really dead, said he was a bird that died in the fire but raised up living again, like the Cherokee people. I lifted my head then, but it wasn't Floyd. It was a tiny little Indian boy in red and white feathers sitting on a big shield. Those false Cherokees with their thick fat black braids were holding the shield high in the air, dancing around, and the music was roaring, and it might've been a real Indian kid they were holding, and it might've meant to stand for all Indian people, and it might've meant to be hopeful and a lot of things—but to me, Floyd was my son, and he was just as dead.

I never looked at that stage anymore.

AFTERWARDS we went back to Floyd's house for a party. He was living with some white boys in an apartment complex with a swimming pool out front. Those kids were all every one drunk. Floyd was drinking bad himself, drinking murderous. Drinking bad as I drank the first months after I found out Floyd's daddy was killed. And those white kids were all every one the same, laying around on each other and jumping in the swimming pool with their clothes on and one boy buck naked with no clothes on at all, and squealing and laughing and the music loud. They treated Floyd like a pet. They liked him, you could tell that—they liked how good he could dance, they thought he was a star—but they acted towards him like he was some kind of little monkey or pet coyote or something, like they couldn't believe he was so smart and could do so many tricks. They didn't know what to make of me. One or two of them come up to where I was sitting at the kitchen table and said, so, you're Floyd's mother. That was it. Like they couldn't think of anything else that made sense to say after that.

Delores and me finally left. We watched Floyd drinking and squealing around some himself and being treated so by these white kids, and him not even able to tell, I guess, that it wasn't any different from coming up Quanah Avenue with the little kids swarming and teasing—it just felt different to him because now he was the pet. So we left and drove home to Tulsa. We got there when the sky was starting to turn light.

I WENT back to Tahlequah one other time. I wanted to see where he went off the side of the mountain. I knew where it was, saw the place in my mind the minute Delores come to the back door and said she'd got a call on the telephone, said it was some bad news. But I wanted to go see it. I'd had them bring Floyd back to Tulsa and we buried him in a cemetery over here by Red Fork. I didn't bury him out south of Tahlequah where his daddy's folks are buried because I didn't want to go back to that town then, because I couldn't. I think about that sometimes now.

But for months and months after Floyd passed on, a picture kept coming to me of this one blacktop curve on the side of a mountain east of Tahlequah. I knew that's where it was. I used to drive out there with Joe. You could park there and sit. You could see all off for miles, south and east, the whole of Baron Fork Valley and off towards Stilwell and all over the hills of the Cherokee country. And I kept thinking about it and thinking about it, and finally Delores

said, well, why don't we just go. So, six or seven months after he was
gone, Delores come got me one morning, and we went back.

The sick feeling slid over me as soon as we topped the hill west
of town, same as I expected, but I just tolerated it and had Delores
drive on. We cut across Muskogee and up through the park and
kept on straight east, and I kept my eyes straight ahead. Out east
of town we started to cross over Highway 10 and the river, heading
on towards the place where Floyd and them went off the mountain,
but I thought of something and had Delores stop and back up. She
turned north like I asked, driving alongside the Illinois River, the
way Highway 10 hugs it, and then we turned off at Sparrow Hawk.

We drove down the dirt road to the riverbed and stopped and got
out. Everything was changed. I walked along the gravel bar and looked
around, but I couldn't recognize anything. For one thing there was
a building there, a kind of shack, a business set up to rent canoes to
tourists so they could float down the Illinois, and there was people
around and two pickups out front with trailers behind them stacked
with canoes marked on the side SPARROW HAWK FLOAT TRIPS. And
the water was green now, greener than ever I remembered, and there
was places along the rocks where white foam swirled in little whirl-
pools, and it was low, flowing slow southwards toward Tenkiller Dam.

But mostly it was the river itself that had changed things. A river
won't ever let the land around it stay the same. I stood at the edge of
the water and looked north where the river was flowing from, and
all the bends and turns were completely changed. Where the water
had one time curved east and swept against an overhanging dirt bank
on the other side where white boys used to reach down their hands
to noodle for catfish, now it curved back the other direction, curved
west, and that bank was washed away, wasn't anything but a slow
stubbly slope to a little strip of sand. I turned and looked downriver,
and the wide sweep of gravel bar where we used to park so many

cars, used to forty-nine, used to camp sometimes with Floyd's daddy's family, was under the water. You could see the highwater mark,
clustered leaves and plastic bags and old sticks and brickle, halfway
up the trees alongside the bank—only that didn't used to be the
bank but a bunch of small river willows and saplings we used to go
off into away from the singing and the fire. They weren't saplings
now. They were trees.

I pointed to the water, to the place under the water, and said to
Delores, "Your daddy gave me Floyd there."

Because it was true. One night camped out in a green U.S. Army
tent, and I didn't care—I left anyhow. I took Delores and moved to
Tulsa, and Joe followed us and begged me, but I still wouldn't, because
I couldn't, because . . . I don't know why. You can't say what jams that
wadding down your throat, what makes you go cold like that inside.
Why Floyd let them white kids taunt him. Why him and Delores
was the ones that died. And their daddy. Joe left Oklahoma then, he
followed his family to California and got run over on a night road
outside Sacramento not even a year later. His brother wrote and told
me. That's the last time I heard from any of them. I never tried to
find them, find out where they lived.

I looked at the water sliding slow over the hidden bed of rocks and
sand and gravel, watched it bending weed stalks growing up stub-
born from the bottom, rippling v's around black branches like snakes'
heads, and then I looked up at the rock cliffs above us called Sparrow
Hawk that the river couldn't change in twenty-two years but maybe
in twenty-two hundred, and that old squeezed-up longing come on
me again. I turned to Delores and pointed at the water and said it
again like she never heard me, "Your daddy gave me Floyd there."

She looked at me, and her face moved.

I turned my eyes back to the river.

There, under the water, the picture of the blacktop curve east of

Tahlequah come to me again, wavering just below the surface. Only now it wasn't anything like when I was a girl. Now the trees were all grown up tall so you couldn't see across the valley and the hills beyond. Now green tops of pines and mottled scrub oaks blocked out the way, except for one place where the guardrail was torn off and there was a great gash down the side of the mountain—and in that one spot you could see.

It turned night on me then, and I saw, like I'd seen it so many times, the car filled with Indian boys going off the side of the mountain and turning and crashing and bursting into fire like in a movie, because it wasn't those white dancers Floyd died with but four other Cherokee boys headed down to the Baron Fork to a forty-nine. I put my hand out to stop it. I might've cried out. I wanted to call everything back. And the image wouldn't stop but went on and on like it had and would in the endlessness of earth's memory, until at last, of its own will, it turned light again and shimmered. And I felt the old grief and gratitude he'd gone back Cherokee before he died.

I stood then, in the light, in that place on the side of the mountain and looked through the gash in the treetops like I stood at the top of the earth turning, and everything heaved up inside me, the longing tightened and squeezed up inside me, and I looked out at the circle of hills and the water and the place that was inside my blood's memory that I couldn't ever get out or away from in my heart forever.

I just looked a long time.

Ritual

2009

It's not the end of the world, Aradhna told herself. It's just global warming. Driving west she scanned the hills for their usual fall fury, but the Catskills rolled on toward the horizon in wan shades of tan and ochre. The sugar maples hadn't burst into flame with the first frost. There'd been no frost. Some of the trees were fading to beige or yellow; others had offered up a feeble khaki sigh before shedding their leaves entirely in the lingering warmth. On either side of the blacktop, the cornstalks nodded a pale neurasthenic green. She drove on past the abandoned dairy, the stagnant pewter pond where Woodstock hippies had famously bathed naked forty years before, on toward the festival site, where she would sit cross-legged on the monument and burn sage and sweetgrass in Kimmy's memory, before rushing home in time to meet the plumber. It was hard to think of frozen pipes on a day like this, the sun beating hot on her arm through the car window, but even in the throes of climate change, Aradhna believed, sooner or later, in Sullivan County, winter would come.

When she spied the van in the parking area, she almost kept driving. An old white Econoline with Arkansas plates, bug-spattered, road-filmed. She thought about coming back after the plumber finished draining the pipes, but it would be late then, almost dark, and anyway she still had too much left to do—cancel the propane, unplug the

120

phone, load the car, the two-hour drive to the city, or more likely three. Why on earth had she agreed to meet David for dinner at seven? The traffic was going to be horrible. Aradhna downshifted into second, trying to ignore the slick knot of dread in her stomach. She had to do this right now or she'd never do it. The Subaru's shocks thumped as she drove over the low ditch, parked on the far side of the van. A shaggy-haired figure slouched behind the steering wheel. Sleeping. Well, that was good. If the driver was here, maybe the monument area was clear. Aradhna glanced that direction, but the landscaping shrubs blocked her view. Well hell. She grabbed the leather satchel from the floorboard, shoved open the car door.

The guy in the van slept on as she made her way past and into the labyrinth of yews, from which she emerged seconds later to find the long sweep of field sparkling a bizarre, brilliant green in late autumn and a barefoot girl in a tie-dyed skirt kneeling on the woodchips in front of the concrete slab. Great, Aradhna thought. A bippie. Her word for the baby hippies. She started to reverse course, but the girl scrambled to her feet. "Oh hi. Do you work here?"

Aradhna stopped. "No, I'm just . . . looking."

"Oh. Me too." The girl returned her gaze to the names on the plaque. Richie Havens. Creedence Clearwater Revival. Santana. Canned Heat. These young retro hippies were baffling. They'd been born decades after Woodstock, yet they made the pilgrimage here the same as the old graybeards, stood gazing at the names with the same kind of veneration. Aradhna slipped her phone from her jeans pocket, checked the bright blue digits. Maybe she could out-wait the girl.

"That's not all of them, you know," the girl said. "It don't list Bert Sommer or the Keef Hartley Band. What's that tell you?" Aradhna said nothing. Conversation would just make the kid hang around longer. "Tells *me* the ones that put up this plaque wasn't really here," the girl said.

Aradhna smiled a tight little smile, began to dig around in her satchel.

"Where was the stage—do you know?"

Aradhna pointed to the low area at the foot of the hill. She quickly lowered her hand.

"Yeah. That's what I was thinking. From the pictures." The girl stared down at the plaque again. "They spelled John Sebastian's name wrong. That's dumb. Sebastian's not tricky. Everybody spells my name wrong. It's Faythe. F-A-Y-T-H-E, but people always want to spell it F-A-I-T-H. Like Blind Faith. Did you ever see them? I'm Faythe, my next sister's Hope, and the baby's Courtney. For Courtney Love? That was my Nan's idea, so we'd be like Faythe, Hope, and Love, sort of. Pretty cheesy, right? What's yours?"

"My what? Oh. Mary," Aradhna said.

"Mary as in Mother of God or Merry as in Merry Christmas?"

"The former."

"What?"

"Mary as in Mother of God."

"I had a friend in fifth grade named Merry like Merry Christmas." The girl moved to the far side of the monument and perched there, surveying the field with her chin in her hand. "Can we camp here?"

"No." Aradhna glanced toward the museum offices at the top of the hill. "It's private property. Look, are you going to be here long?"

The girl shrugged. "A while I guess. Do you know where we could camp? We drove straight through from Springdale, or Ramon did. I don't drive yet. Well, I think I *could* drive, but he don't trust me. Now looks like he's fixing to sleep all day, but that's okay. It wasn't his idea to come here, his idea was to go straight on to Maine. How far is it to Maine?"

"Quite a ways."

"Well, we'd better camp somewhere around here then."

"The campsites are all closed now. The season's over. You'll have to get a motel."

"No," the girl said. "We can't do that. Wow!" She jumped up and rushed forward so fast, Aradhna took a step back. "That is so cool," the girl said, reaching for the satchel. "It looks Indian. Is it Indian?"

"I don't know." Aradhna pulled the satchel to her chest, a reflex. "It was a gift."

"Can I see?"

Reluctantly Aradhna allowed the girl to touch the beadwork.

"God, it's beautiful. Is it, like, a medicine wheel or something?"

"I think it's supposed to be a mandala." The girl looked blank. "A mandala," Aradhna said. "Sort of a picture of the cosmos . . . or like an image of the unity of the universe. Some people use them for meditation . . ." It felt too complicated to explain.

"Oh," Faythe said, disappointed, dropping her hand away from the bag. "That kind of Indian. Ramon's part Indian. Not India Indian, Mexico Indian." She turned and walked back to the fence, stood staring over the field, her face flushed. She didn't look the same as other bippics Aradhna had seen. Those kids adopted to eerie perfection the washed-out, straight-haired, back-to-the-land look. Whenever she happened upon them, here at the site, or pumping gas in White Lake, Aradhna always felt as if she'd stepped into a time warp. She could be looking at any of her friends from her own youth. This girl, though, was too dramatic. Her features were too bold, her eyelashes too long and lush. She wore the costume of forty years ago, but the small silver stud in the side of her nose and the elaborate tattoo snaking from her T-shirt sleeve told the generation she came from. "What's that out there?" The girl pointed. "It looks like a cross or something."

"It's a totem pole."

"What's that sticking out on the sides then?"

"I think they're supposed to be wings."

Faythe turned to Aradhna. "But a totem pole's Indian, right?"

"Well, not exactly. Or not that one. A friend of mine carved it. Ed Schmidt. He's definitely not Native."

"A friend of yours? You live here?"

"Part of the time. Or I . . ." She started to say *used to*, but the words wouldn't quite come.

"If Indians didn't carve it, what's it doing here?"

"It's sort of a memorial. To the dead."

"The Grateful Dead?"

Despite herself, Aradhna laughed. "Actually, Garcia is one of them. It's a marker for the ones who played here in '69 and have passed on. Jimi Hendrix, Janis Joplin. And yeah, Jerry Garcia from the Grateful Dead. You can see their faces if you go to the other side."

"Can we do that?"

Aradhna started to shake her head no, then she thought, oh, snap. "Why, sure," she said brightly. "Just go right through the fence there and hike down. Nobody cares." The girl stepped toward the fence, stopped, and looked back. Aradhna smiled at her. "You don't want to come all this way and miss the best part."

The girl flashed a glance toward the parking area. "Ramon might wake up."

"If he does, I'll show him where you are. Go on." Aradhna waved her open hands, shooing the girl forward. Faythe stared at her a moment. "My Nan does that," she said, and turned to slip through the fence slats, walked away down the field.

Your Nan, Aradhna thought. As in Nana. As in Grandma. Surely not. Aradhna frowned, took a long breath, looked around. At least the monument area felt private, closed off from the road by the suffocating yews, though open on the far side to the long field, where she could see the girl's figure receding. In the woodchip-strewn lot, the slab sat just off center like a great flat tombstone inscribed with too many names. Aradhna edged toward it, digging in the satchel as she went. She withdrew a clean jar lid, a Ziploc baggie of dried sage, a framed color photograph of a blonde woman spreadeagled on this same monument, flashing the peace sign with both hands. Aradhna placed the items on the slab's surface. She tapped a little hill of sage into the lid and set it in front of the picture, then she dug out a dog-eared book of matches. Striking match after match, she held the lit ends to the sage till it caught and smoldered. She crawled onto the monument, sat cross-legged, leaned over, and bathed herself in the smoke, scooping it toward her face, pouring it over her hair with both hands. She paused, staring at the laughing face.

"Hey, girlfriend," she said. "I'm back. I know I'm early. Not as early as you might think, though. It's just hot as hell. Things are really . . . different this year." She wiped sweat from her upper lip, gazing out over the strange landscape—the trees leached of color, the grass fantastically green. Every year since Kimmy's death, Aradhna had come here to mark the date, but last December, as she'd sat shivering on the icy slab beneath a cold sleety rain, she'd made up her mind to change from Kimmy's death date to the date of her birth: her August birthday. In August, though, the site had been swarming with tourists. In August there had also been David. It had felt too complicated, too soon. Too something. Aradhna had put it off till September. But that was when the rains came; there'd been terrible flooding, roads washed out, mold crawling the walls, and after that a crushing heat wave that had left her house smelling like sin. She'd spent most of October in the city with David. He was there full-time now; he'd sold the house—his and Kimmy's—had started talking about moving inland, getting out of New York, away from the coast. Somewhere safe, he said. Safe, Aradhna thought. Where's safe?

"Tell you what, Kimmy girl, you split just in time. We've got storms of the century rolling in about once a month now. We got floods and wildfires, melting ice caps, vanishing treefrogs—I could run you a list to make you turn over in your grave. If you had one. Sorry. Bad joke." She reached out to touch the frame. A sudden tremor passed through her, a sense of something enormous taking place, not just here but everywhere, all over the cosmos. "Livingston Manor got swept away by the Willowemoc," she told the picture softly. "People died, Kim. Is that weird? The Willow-*we*-moc, that pretty little stream, it turned lethal . . . oh, shut up. Never mind."

She slid to the edge of the slab, stood and walked around; she started toward the parking area, abruptly turned and came back, snatched up the satchel, reached in and pulled out a braided swatch of dried sweetgrass. She located the matches, lit the sweetgrass, stood in front of the monument with her trembling hands clasped at heart level, her breath coming in short sharp little gasps. Slowly she raised the smoldering grass skyward; she lowered her hands, stood very still, breathing deeply. After a moment she began to turn in a slow circle; at each compass point she paused, raised the smoking sweetgrass high over her head.

"What's that?"

Aradhna whirled. "Jesus, you scared the life out of me!"

"Sorry." Faythe stood outside the fence.

"Don't you know better than to sneak up on people?"

"Sorry," the girl said again. She stared at the burning sweetgrass. "Pisses my Nan off too, when I do that."

"And stop comparing me to your damn grandma!"

"She's not my grandma," the girl said, ducking down to slip through the fence. "She's my aunt."

"Whatever."

"My great-aunt."

"Just stop it!"

"Sure." The girl edged closer. "I guess totem poles are supposed to be gross or something, but if you didn't already tell me who it was, I'd have never guessed. Well, Hendrix maybe, but not the others." She gazed steadily at the objects on the monument. "So, is it going to make you madder if I ask what you're doing? 'Cause I don't want to make you mad."

"I'm not mad."

The girl raised her eyebrows but said nothing.

"I'm enacting a ritual, if you must know—or trying to, if I could get a little goddamn privacy."

"A ritual," the girl said, her tone satisfied, as if the word affirmed something. She picked up the framed photograph. "Who's this?"

"My best friend. Kimmy." Aradhna retrieved the frame, set it back on the slab.

"So, what I was thinking," Faythe said, "we could—hey, don't do that!" she cried out as Aradhna began swatting the sweetgrass against the concrete to put it out. "You don't have to stop. I'll shut up. Really."

"It's too late. I've got to go." Aradhna dumped the blackened sage from the jar lid, tapped the lid to clear it, jammed it back inside the leather bag. She suddenly dropped the satchel, sat down heavily on the concrete slab. She leaned forward and put her head in her hands.

"Mary? Are you okay?"

Aradhna said nothing. Her head was reeling.

"We got some Boost bars and shit in the van. You want something to eat? Mary?" It had been so long since she'd been called by her birth name that it took a second for Aradhna to recognize the girl was talking to her. "You okay?" the girl said again.

"No," Aradhna said. "I don't think you could say I'm okay at all." In the silence she heard for the first time the humming of crickets in the field, or she thought they must be crickets—insects anyway, a thousand tiny voices droning a low resonant hum. They ought to all be dead now. Surely. It's nearly November, for chrissake. She raised her eyes to meet the girl's. "Something weird is going on," she told her.

"No joke," the girl said. She stood with one foot propped on the other, twirling a strand of hair around one finger. After a moment she came and sat down on the slab. "So what's the weirdest thing that's ever happened to you?"

"I don't know," Aradhna said. "I can't remember." Her head was killing her. Maybe she was having a stroke.

"One time me and Nan met my mom at a truck stop near Albuquerque. That was weird. We were driving to Reno to get her, but she didn't know we were coming because there was a power outage or something—I was only seven, I don't remember what the cause was—but what we didn't know, my mom had got tired of waiting and caught a ride back to Arkansas. So me and Nan stopped to get a pop at this trucker place outside Albuquerque, walk in, who's sitting there with her ride, eating pie? My mom. I wasn't surprised then, I just ran and jumped in her lap, but Nan about had a fit. So did my mom. After I grew up, though, I realized how freaky that is—us all stopping at the same ratty truck stop on I-40 on the same day, at the same hour, the same minute, no less. Coming from two different directions." She picked up the blackened sweetgrass from where Aradhna had dropped it, sat rotating the long swatch in her hand. "So," she said after a beat, "did you always love him?"

"Who?"

"Your girlfriend's husband."

"Lord no," Aradhna said.

"But you do now, right?"

"Not really."

"What are you going to marry him for then?"

Aradhna jerked alert. "Why do you say that?"

"Isn't that what you told me?"

"No. Did I?"

The girl shrugged. She sat staring at the emerald field, her fingers absently plucking bits of burnt sweetgrass from the charred braid. Aradhna rubbed her thudding forehead. What was going on here? She hadn't said anything about marrying David, not even to Kimmy, though she had meant to, surely. That's part of what she'd come for. She just hadn't got that far. Had she?

"There's room at the top," Faythe said. "Up above Janis Joplin. If we wait till it gets dark, I don't think they'll stop us. You could go home and get your ladder."

"My what?"

"Your ladder. For us to stand on while we carve out her face."

"Whose face? What are you talking about?"

"My mom. She was born here, you know. Out yonder. In the mud."

"Right," Aradhna said. Even with her brains addled with pain, Aradhna grasped the girl's meaning: the decades-old myth of the baby born at Woodstock. Or was it a myth? Aradhna didn't know, but she was fairly certain the girl had been fed a line of bull by a flaky mother looking to mythologize her own life. She opened her mouth to say something to that effect, but what came out was: "You can't do that. That's defacing private property."

The girl raised her eyebrows. "Not *de*-facing," she said. She stared down the field. "Ramon's a fantastic artist," she said. "He'll do a great job."

"They got security patrolling this place all night. They're not going to just let you carve up that pole."

"They won't see us."

Aradhna glanced over, but the girl was still gazing down the hill, idly scraping the sweetgrass across her bare arm. The charred end made long, faintly gray streaks across her tattoo—a bird-headed

dragon or dragon-tailed phoenix, it was hard to tell which. Aradhna
saw then that it wasn't a real tattoo but a pen-and-ink drawing,
smudged faintly at her sleeve. "Ramon's going to freak," the girl said.
"I told him we'd find the right way." She turned to grin at Aradhna.
"We're not actually on our way to Maine. Where we're really going
is Canada. Ramon thinks Maine might be an easier place to cross."

"Easier than what?" For the first time a wave of real concern pushed
through Aradhna. She eyed the girl closely. "Why do you need to
cross where Ramon thinks it's easy?"

"Just do," the girl said.

"How old are you?" Aradhna looked hard at her, trying to gauge
the answer. Too young for a legal tattoo evidently. So: younger than
eighteen.

"He's not my boyfriend," the girl said, "if that's what you're thinking.
He's more like a brother, you know? His folks live next door to my
Nan, or they did till the ICE people came. We lived there because
my mom went to Wyoming with her new boyfriend. Bear, I think his
name was. Yeah, Bear. He wasn't a drummer or anything, he was like
a biker dude she met in Branson. She said she was going to send for
us when they got settled, and I really think she would have done it
this time, but she got wasp stung on a trail ride last summer. She died."

"Died?" Aradhna said. "Your mother?" The girl nodded. "From a
wasp sting?"

The girl nodded again. "She didn't even know she was allergic. Or
I guess she didn't know. Nan said she didn't. Nan raised my mom
too, same as us. Or sometimes she raised us. Sometimes it was just
us and Mom, traveling around."

Aradhna wanted to ask what had happened to the girl's grandparents, and her father—why wasn't he in the picture? But the story just
seemed too sad, too contemporary-fractured-family, too emblematic

of how everything was falling apart, and she only murmured, "Sorry for your loss."

"Yeah," the girl said softly. "Me too." She lifted her face to the gleaming field. The sun was slanting deep now. After a moment she said, "So how about you? How'd your friend die?"

Aradhna tried to think how to tell what had seemed so senseless, so unnecessary and pointless: how Kimmy had been complaining for a week that she couldn't breathe, but she'd kept putting off going to the doctor because they'd lost their insurance when David went to work for himself; how Aradhna had advised her on the phone to try inhaling Vicks water from a pot on the stove, try some mullein tea; how she'd warned Kimmy against eating wheat or other mucous-producing agents, but had never once said *damn the cost, Kim, what the hell, I'll pay for it, just go to the damn doctor!* as she'd imagined herself saying a thousand times since that frozen night her friend's lungs filled so rapidly, so ruthlessly, that Kimmy couldn't rise from the bed, couldn't talk, and David had frantically phoned for an ambulance, but by the time the medics got there, it was too late. The autopsy report said she'd died from pulmonary edema. It cited no underlying cause. But there is always an underlying cause, Aradhna thought. Always. Aloud she said only, "Kimmy drowned."

Faythe nodded. "Look," she said. "Sun's heading down. Won't be long now."

Aradhna leaned back to dig her phone out of her pocket. "Shit," she said, reading the phone's face.

"What?"

"Nothing. I just missed the plumber." Aradhna snapped the phone closed. "I expect they'll charge me for the damn house call anyway."

"Nope," Faythe said. "I don't think they will." Aradhna pivoted to look at her; pain rocketed through her skull. The girl stood, began to gather Aradhna's things. "We can't do anything till it gets dark anyways," she said, stuffing the picture frame inside the satchel. "We might as well go eat."

Driving toward her house in the purpling dusk, her head throbbing, her vision blurring each time she glanced in the rearview to see the Econoline jouncing along ghostlike behind her, Aradhna considered making a left onto Happy Avenue, driving fast through the twisty-turny backroads until she'd lost them, but she knew she would not. She would take them home, feed them, get her extension ladder from the storage shed, just as Faythe had said, and allow the groggy, shaggy-haired Ramon to lash it to the top of the van. Then she would leave her Subaru parked in the driveway and ride back with them to the festival site. And why? It was not a question she knew how to answer.

She told herself it was because she needed to keep an eye on this Ramon fellow, make sure he wasn't some weird internet pedophile kidnapper or something, but even as he'd sat blinking at her from the van while Faythe introduced her as "*mi nueva amiga* Mary," Aradhna had realized that the guy didn't exactly look like a predator—not that she could have said how a predator should look. What Ramon did look like was a very weary, very thin, slightly grubby boy a bit older than Faythe herself. And yes, he appeared to be Mexican, or Latino anyway, dark-complected, brown-eyed, with that great mop of dark hair. The girl talked to him in a choppy American-accented Spanish, and the boy answered in quick rippling sibilant Spanish, but he didn't say anything to Aradhna—not even later, in her kitchen, when she set a plate of scrambled eggs and a jar of salsa in front of him, though he flashed a shy smile and bobbed his head in thanks before digging in. The one peculiar thing about him, actually, was the fact that the mass of dark hair on his head was a wig. And not an especially good wig either.

Aradhna had realized this as soon as he climbed out of the van in her driveway, and now, beneath the fluorescent kitchen lights, the fact was even more obvious. She could see where the nylon strands were sewn to the netting along the part line. The shaggy thing was hardly better than a Halloween fright wig, and it embarrassed her for the boy, and that alone, even if he hadn't been so hungry and so slight, probably accounted for why she felt more pity than concern. Both kids, in fact, were ravenous. Faythe's plate was already half empty, and the boy was sopping up picante sauce with one of the waffles Aradhna had dug out of the freezer and toasted. She didn't have any butter to offer them, no syrup. She was sorry now that she'd already cleaned out the fridge, had kept only the carton of free-range eggs she was bringing to David.

David. Damn. No way was she going to make it to the city by seven. Aradhna pulled out her phone, started to speed dial his number, but then she stopped, looked over at the two young people finishing off their eggs in concentrated silence, and instead stepped into the pantry and took down a jar of gourmet tomato bisque soup and a can of baked beans. Moments later, when she heard David's scratchy ringtone, she pushed the mute button on the phone, jammed it back in her pocket. Glancing up, she found Faythe's eyes steady on her, but the girl immediately turned to scan the cramped, bright kitchen. "Looks like y'all just quit on this place," she said, chewing.

Aradhna followed the girl's gaze from the grimy plateless light switch to the unvarnished baseboards to the half-spackled gypsum along the north wall. "I suppose you could put it that way," she said airily and turned to open the jar of soup. She didn't care to think about the unfinished kitchen just now, or anything else that had to do with Jerry—the abandoned mud room, the never-even-started solarium, all the empty plans they'd made sitting by the woodstove in winter. Aradhna had not spent a full winter here since the divorce.

Building fires no longer seemed cozy and romantic; it seemed la-
bor-intensive and dirty. She scraped soup from the bottom of the
jar into the saucepan. "It's hard to stay on top of things. I don't live
here all the time."

"You should," the girl said.

Aradhna shot her a glance, but the girl was reaching across the
table for a waffle. Aradhna plunked bowls of soup and baked beans
in front of them and went to sit in the darkened living room while
the kids ate. She turned on the television, forgetting until she saw
the drifting icon that David had taken down the satellite dish. She
clicked off the remote, sat staring out the patio doors at the fireflies
blinking in the yard. Fireflies in October. Jesus. A seasonal perver-
sion as weird as the mice hordes swarming in all last summer. That
invasion had been so overwhelming, Aradhna had switched from
the live traps she'd been using for years to the old-fashioned snap-
their-furry-little-necks type, thinking maybe it was the same released
mice coming in over and over. But each morning there would be
new mouse pills in her silverware drawer, more dead mice in the
traps, their shiny black eyes shocked open, their tiny paws trapped
under the metal guillotine, reaching for the smear of peanut butter
on the bait plate. She'd slaughtered probably a couple hundred over
the course of the summer, but now, when it had supposedly turned
autumn, the season when field mice usually come in looking for a
warm place to winter, she hadn't seen a single tiny turd in any drawer,
not one flicker of gray whisking along a baseboard. Maybe I wiped
them all out, she thought. A wave of despair passed over her, and
she got up and went to the glass doors, drew the shades.

She curled up on the love seat in the dark, listening to the kids'
voices in the kitchen, quick and hushed, unintelligible, like a radio in
the next room turned too low. Were they arguing? She couldn't tell.
People talking fast in Spanish always sounded to her like a fight. If so,

it was surely nothing like the shouting, door-slamming, wall-punch-
ing fights she and Jerry used to have. Or the ones Kimmy described
having with David. Those two fought like hell, Aradhna thought, and
the two of us fought like hell, but for entirely opposite reasons. Well,
no, actually, it was for a lot of the same reasons—money, mostly—
but Kimmy and David fought because he was such a tightwad, and
Aradhna and Jerry fought because he was so reckless—with money,
yes, but also with time, energy, her emotions, and he never finished
any goddamn thing he started, except the affair with the Large Child,
as Aradhna called the twenty-something redhead he'd left her for
three years ago. Aradhna snorted in the dark. That was her main re-
gret about getting married again, how it let Jerry off the hook—he
could quit paying alimony.

One thing about it, she and David never argued. Well, only once,
and you could hardly call it an argument. She'd gotten a bit testy,
that's all, when he'd said she should go ahead and list her house.
What if it sold before she was ready? Where would she store her
stuff until they moved wherever they were moving? Fat chance in
this lousy market, he'd muttered, and motioned the waiter to bring
the check. They'd left the restaurant in silence. Ordinarily, though,
they were extremely polite with each other. Hell, we don't even know
each other well enough to fight, Aradhna thought. The girl's question echoed: *What are you going to marry him for then?* Irritably she
groped for the remote, pointed it at the TV, clicked. She watched
the bright blue letters materialize on the black screen. Kimmy was
right about David and money. He could be generous, actually, in
some ways, but there was also something small and pinched about
him, parsimonious. Like how he'd unscrewed the satellite dish from
the roof last Sunday and taken it with him to the city wrapped in
bubble wrap. "You won't be here to use it," he'd said. "We'll take it
with us when we move; that way we won't have to buy a new one in

Illinois." Or was it Indiana? Ohio? Iowa. One of the vowel states in the middle of the country. Her eyes followed the wandering cobalt image. *Searching for satellite signal* it said, meandering, seeking its source. Lost. Like Kimmy, she thought.

"If you outlive me, Buster," Kimmy had wagged her finger at David one evening at dinner, "you'd better not bury me in this freaking cold Catskill ground." She was a Southern girl, a Floridian, and she'd threatened to haunt her husband forever if he buried her here in Sullivan County. And he hadn't. He'd carried her ashes to Tampa and cast her into the warm Gulf waters, as Kimmy probably wanted. But now she is nowhere, Aradhna thought. She told herself she understood why her friend didn't want to be buried here. She'd made her own brother promise years ago to bring her home and plant her in Oklahoma no matter where she finally croaked. But not wanting to be buried in the north country is not the same as not wanting to be buried at all. One's body vanished to ash and smoke, drifting on the wind, the salty sea, dissolved. Ashes to ashes, dust to dust. A shudder passed through her. Abruptly she stood and bumped through the dark living room, calling out, "Are you kids about finished?"

When she reached the doorway she stopped, staring down at the beige tablecloth on the kitchen table. For an instant she had the disorienting sense that Kimmy's face had materialized there, like Jesus's face in the Shroud of Turin. The face on the cloth was so perfectly life-sized, so stunningly lifelike, she could almost hear Kimmy's laugh. In the next instant she realized that Ramon had been sketching the drawing onto the cloth in ballpoint pen. "What are you doing? You can't do that!" She rushed into the room and snatched up the framed photograph he was using for a model. Then she sat down heavily in a chair, the frame clasped to her chest, and began to weep—softly at first, then more and more violently, until she was heaving in great ragged sobs. In a moment she felt the girl's hand lightly patting her shoulder; she shrugged the hand off, though without anger. Gradually, very slowly her sobs began to ebb.

"I hunted around for some paper," Faythe said. Her voice sounded apologetic. "We tried a paper towel, but it tore. Ramon wanted to practice. Hey, we got a Tide pen in the van. If that ink don't come out, we'll get you a new one, okay? Mary?"

Aradhna tried to control her breathing. "My name isn't Mary," she said. There was a beat of silence. She could hear her pulse thumping in her own ears. She kept her gaze on the boy across the table; he didn't meet her eyes but went on fiddling restlessly with the ballpoint pen.

"What is it then?" Faythe said.

"Aradhna."

"A-rah—what?"

"Aradhna. It means 'worship' in Hindi. I chose it when I decided to change my life."

Another moment of silence. "How'd you do that? Change your life?"

Dear God. What a question. Aradhna filtered her attempts over the years, the various means of seeking truth, enlightenment, whatever the hell it had been, starting with transcendental meditation way back in her youth; that was when she'd changed her name, tried to follow the teachings of the Maharishi Mahesh Yogi, like the Beatles. But the slowness of TM irritated her, and she'd switched to Silva Mind Control—total commercial bullshit, she'd come to see, which was probably why she'd never tried est. She did become a Baha'i for a couple of years, back in the seventies, then a Zen Buddhist, or so she'd told people if they asked. She'd read a lot about Buddhism in those years anyway. Ultimately, she had settled into a moderately consistent practice of lacto-ovo-vegetarianism and hatha yoga. "I quit eating meat," she said.

"That's cool," the girl said. "Look. We got to go soon. The moon'll

be rising. Here, don't forget this." Faythe picked up the beaded satchel
and placed it in her arms.

SOMETHING about the van's phlegmy motor, its smell, the darkness
surrounding her, soothed Aradhna on the ride over. She felt calm
now, relieved; her head was no longer aching. She sat in the back
seat, leaning forward between the two young people to see the road.
The van didn't smell of weed and patchouli, as she'd half expected
when she climbed in, but like oily rags and cold metal, a smell like
her father's work truck. Her throat tightened. They'd been gone such
a long time, her parents. She felt the need to explain her weeping
outburst. "My husband moved out the same month Kimmy died;
it's coming up on the anniversary. I guess it just all hit me at once."

"Hey, no problem," Faythe said. "I totally freaked when they told me
my mom was dead. I still do sometimes, if I think about it too much."
Yes, Aradhna thought, but your mom died last summer. My shit
happened three years ago. I should get over it already. Aloud she
said, "Take a left here."

"*Izquierda*," Faythe told Ramon.

Aradhna guided them along the country roads, approaching the
festival site from the back way. She told Faythe to tell Ramon to
kill the lights when they were still a quarter mile from the site; they
coasted along in the dark, parked on the shoulder. Ramon unlashed
the fiberglass ladder, handed it down over the side of the van, and
soon the three of them were lugging it along the quiet road, stumbling from time to time in the darkness, Aradhna at the front, leading
the way. They crossed the black sweep of field in silence. The security
lights around the pavilions at the top of the hill gave just enough
illumination to let them see where they were going, but not enough,
Aradhna hoped, to reveal their silhouettes to the security patrol.

Even at a distance the totem pole seemed taller, more formidable than she remembered. It's because of the darkness, Aradhna told herself. They drew near the pole's base, and Aradhna, looking up, thought how the carved outspread wings, which had always reminded her goofily of Farrah Fawcett's hair, seemed from this angle authentic, apt for their purpose. It does look a bit like a crucifix, she thought. The idea gave her the willies, and she quickly plunked her end of the ladder on the ground with a grunt. Ramon at once hoisted his end and set it firmly against the pole. He took the small canvas bag Faythe held out and slipped his hand through the tie-string, scrambled nimbly to the upper rungs. Aradhna listened to the sound of her own huffing and puffing from the trek across the field. The girl was a silent dark shadow beside her. In time, as her heaving slowed, Aradhna began to hear soft little thumps coming from the top of the ladder, followed by the sound of scraping, occasional soft snuffles like a hand brushing across wood. How can he see well enough to know what he's doing? she wondered.

"Ramon knows my mom's face so good he could draw it blindfolded," Faythe said.

"Quit that!" Aradhna snapped.

"What?" the girl whispered.

"Acting like you goddamn know what I'm thinking," Aradhna whispered back.

The girl answered nothing. The soft little scrapes and thuds continued overhead.

"I'm sorry," Aradhna said after a moment.

"It's okay. I don't do it on purpose. I just think shit and say it and half the time somebody'll say, how'd you know that? I used to believe it made me special. But then I got older and found out it just made me weird."

"You're not weird," Aradhna said, without conviction.

"Reckon I am."

Aradhna suppressed an urge to pat the girl's shoulder; instead, she muttered, "Looks like this is going to take awhile. We might as well sit down."

The grass was damp with dew. The two sat at the foot of the pole, facing the direction where the original festival stage had been. The whole field was alive with fireflies, their bodies igniting, dancing a short distance, blinking out. Got to be a hundred thousand of them, Aradhna thought. A million.

"It's like a rock concert," Faythe breathed. "Where everybody flicks on their cigarette lighters and holds 'em up?"

"It's weird is what it is," Aradhna said. "You're supposed to see fireflies in June, not the end of October."

"Yeah. I guess. Maybe it's people's souls. Maybe it's all the dead hippies dancing in the dark."

"Oh, hush."

"Don't you believe in souls?"

Aradhna didn't answer. She didn't know what she believed anymore.

"I do," Faythe said. "I think my mom's here this minute. If she was ever going to sit still someplace, it'd be here. She wouldn't sit, though. She'd be like those lightning bugs, flitting around. Blinking on. Blinking off. Think about it. She could have been born right on this very spot where we're sitting. Our whole lives she talked about coming back, it was like this big dream she had. Nan said that it was just a notion my mom got about herself because she was born in 1969 and her mama died when she was little, and she never had a dad, so she made up that story on account of we had that tape of the Woodstock movie and my mom watched it a bazillion times. It's not true though. What Nan said. My mother *was* born here. I can feel it."

Aradhna shivered. It was hard not to believe her.

"I wish I still had some of her ashes. I'd bury them right under this pole. Nan took them up to the Christ of the Ozarks and threw them off the mountain. That is so not fair. Just because Nan turned into a Jesus freak don't mean my mom did." The girl raised her face and called up softly, "How's it going?"

"*Bien.*" The boy's voice seemed to float from an echo chamber. "Few minutes more."

"He speaks English?"

"Sure. He came up from Jalisco, like, two years ago. He's just shy is all. It's weird though, isn't it? My mom traveled practically all over the whole country, but she never came back here. That's one thing I don't want to happen to me—live your whole life thinking you're going to do something, planning it, talking about it, really believing that one of these days you're going to do it, and then you get stung by a wasp in Wyoming."

"Well," Aradhna said. She began to fidget, wanting to do something. Smoke a joint. Turn on a TV. She plucked a damp blade of grass and rolled it between her fingers. What kind of thing was it she'd wanted her whole life that was never going to happen? Enlightenment, she used to think. Peace. Well, not so much peace, probably, as a peaceful identity. She'd always thought she'd get that someday. She used to tell people she wanted to see Africa, although which country in Africa she'd never settled on. They all seemed so dangerous now. Wars and rumors of wars, child soldiers, famine, AIDS, Ebola, kwashiorkor.

"Listen." Faythe touched her arm. High overhead the faint honking of geese sounded—distant at first, growing louder, nearer, until the excited cacophony passed directly above them in the black sky, faded away into the distance. "Wow. That was cool. What was it, ducks?"

"Canada geese. Flying south for the winter."

"At night?"

"They do that sometimes. Usually when the moon's shining."

"How come they're headed north then?"

The flock had indeed been flying from south to north—a bizarre inversion, Aradhna thought. Although no more bizarre than the rest of things, surely. "They're looking for a body of water to land on, I guess."

"Hey, maybe it's a sign. Me and Ramon are going north for the winter."

"Yeah, I wanted to talk to you about that. You know you're not going to be able to just walk across the border."

"Ramon says we can."

"Trust me. Ramon doesn't know."

"He's crossed the other border bunches of times, and that's desert. Woods in Maine can't be so bad."

"And how old are you?"

"Sixteen."

"Right."

"On my next birthday."

"Which is?"

"July ninth."

"How old is Ramon?" The girl didn't answer. "Is he over eighteen?" Faythe nodded. "Over twenty-one?" The girl blinked, her eyes on the ground. Aradhna sighed. "If you care about him, I mean whatsoever, you'll make him turn that van around tomorrow morning and take you home."

"We can't."

"Why not?" No answer again. "Faythe, listen to me. They'll arrest him for kidnapping, they'll put him away for years. Decades. And then they'll deport him."

"But they can't do that! It was my idea."

"Doesn't matter. You're underage, and he's an adult, and Mexican to boot. And illegal, too, if I'm not mistaken. What century do you think you're living in? They'll get him on immigration charges, kidnapping charges, statutory rape—"

"It's not like that!"

"—God knows what else. Homeland security violations, if they can find a way to do it."

"They're not going to see us."

"Like hell."

Faythe stood up and walked away into the dark field.

Ramon called from overhead: "Faythe! *¿A dónde vas?*"

"Shhh!" Aradhna hissed up at him. "You'll alert the patrol!" The boy skittered down the ladder and would have started across the field, but Aradhna stopped him with a hand on his arm. "She's all right. She's just pissed off right now, she'll be back. Listen, Ramon. I need to talk to you. I can't make her hear me, but maybe you can, and I know you understand English, so you don't need to act like you don't. You cannot take that girl to Canada. It's not like you're going to drive though some lily-white Maine border town and not attract any attention. The two of you stick out like a couple of goddamn radishes. Besides which, what would you do up there? How are you going to make a living, buy food, get a place to stay?"

"My cousin have work for me in Montreal—he got a restaurant."

"Well, that's nice. You go work for him if you can get there, but you can't take that girl. She has to go home to her family. She's fifteen years old."

"She will not go."

"Why not? What the hell's this *we cain't do that* bullshit?" Aradhna imitated the girl's twang.

"*Porqué* . . . her aunt, few weeks ago, she drive up to the big Jesus statue and put her mother on the ground, she spreaded out her . . . *cenizas.*"

"Her ashes."

The boy nodded. "And so Faythe make a fire in the yard, and she put in everything from her mother and many things from her aunt

too, and the aunt is very mad, and they have a big fight, and the
firemen come, and the police come, and her aunt say to the police
to put Faythe in the jail."

"Good God, did they do that?"

"No, but she was almost the whole night at the police, and now
her aunt say she will go to the church school or she will go to the
reform school, and these are her choices."

"Oh man."

"So when I have my trouble, Faythe say we go together to my
cousin restaurant, but first she like to come here. So we come here."

"What kind of trouble?"

Faythe's voice came out of the nearby darkness. "They beat the
shit out of him is what kind of trouble. They practically scalped him."
She walked in close enough for Aradhna to make out her features.
Her face was scrunched with crying, or maybe it was anger, because
she was grinding out the words: "They got him down on the ground
and kicked him till his ribs broke and then they cut off his hair with
a pocketknife and made his head bleed."

"Who?"

"Bunch of rednecks driving around Springdale hunting a beaner
to beat up. That's what they told him. And then when he was home
tore up in bed, the ICE men raided the chicken plant and put his
brothers and his uncle and two cousins in jail and they're fixing to
ship them to Mexico and we are not going back to Arkansas so you
can just quit talking about it. We are going to do what we came to
do and then we're driving up to Maine, and you can just come with
us or not."

"Come with you! What makes you think I'd do that?"

"I don't know." The girl's fury seemed to dissipate all at once; she
leaned against the pole, her voice faint. "It's no accident you showed

up here, is all I know. I was thinking maybe you're supposed to come with us."

"Hardly," Aradhna said. "I've got things to do."

"Like what? Marry your friend's husband who you don't even like so you can be miserable till it's too late to do anything about it, like my Nan?"

"No!"

"What then?"

And because she had no answer, Aradhna was almost relieved to hear a vehicle roar to life near the museum at the top of the hill. All three of them turned to see a pair of headlights blink on in the circle drive. They watched the white SUV move slowly beneath the security light, head toward the main road.

"Crap," Faythe said. "You think they heard us?"

"I don't know. Sit. Ramon, put that ladder on the ground. Y'all get down low. We'll lie still and hope they don't come this way."

"There's no road out to here, is there?"

"Just tracks. Hush now."

They lay in a row, pressing their backs into the wet grass, listening to one another's sharp breaths as the security car drove past in the distance along Hurd Road, made a right at the corner and turned into the parking area near the monument. Within moments a flashlight beam was arcing around the yews, sweeping left to right, up and down, until it vanished suddenly, like a spook light snuffed out, and in a moment they heard the motor start up again. The SUV continued east a little way, turned onto the access road at the foot of the hill near the old stage site. Then the headlights started climbing toward them. "Oh Jesus," Aradhna said.

"Be cool," Faythe whispered, and Aradhna snorted. "What?" the girl said.

"Nothing," Aradhna said. But she was back in Oklahoma at a beer bust in a wheat field watching four patrol cars coming fast along a dirt lane, and suddenly her friends were scattering like crows and she was running into the field with them to lie down flat in the tall, damp, sweet-smelling wheat with a spotlight sweeping back and forth overhead and her date, Ricky Reed, pressing against her back, whispering, *Be cool, Be cool*, until the cops came tramping through the wheat and hoisted them up by the elbows and hauled them out of the field and into the cruisers and down to the station and charged them with trespassing and underage drinking and made them all call their parents, and at first she'd refused, sobbing, the Maybelline Velvet Black stinging her eyes, making the tears worse, until the desk sergeant said, "You don't call 'em, little lady, you'll be spending the night in the drunk tank, and believe me, it don't smell nice like the powder room in that country club your daddy belongs to," and she'd said, "My dad works the pipeline," and the desk cop snorted, "Suit yourself," and so she'd called her dad and he'd showed up with his tired, baffled eyes, but it was her mother who grounded her for the rest of the summer, the freaking end of the world, she'd thought, and she'd threatened to run away so many times, but she hadn't, she'd stayed in the house and watched soap operas and gained eleven pounds, and when school started in September, she'd joined the Key Club, a good kid, a better kid than ever. The only time in her life she'd ever been arrested. A wave of giddiness surged through her. She suddenly had a vision of herself in the van driving through the night toward Canada, the kids asleep in the back. She'd be their protector, their den mother, their smuggler. She started to laugh.

"What?" the girl said again.

Aradhna tried to hold in the laughter, but it was like something had burst in her throat; she jammed her knuckles against her lips, giggling convulsively, nearly choking, as the SUV rumbled nearer, the headlights bouncing with the ruts, until it passed by so close Aradhna couldn't believe the guard didn't see them. But he was steering straight ahead; she could see his dash-lit profile peering up toward the performance pavilion and museum on the hilltop—sites more likely for trespassers and vandals than the crude totem pole standing in the middle of the field. Even after the SUV cleared the hill and the sound of the engine faded, the three lay motionless, looking up at the jeweled sky, star-dusted now, no moonlight. Aradhna sighed a shuddery breath into the silence. "I wanted to run away one time."

"Where'd you go?" Faythe said.

"Oh, I didn't run. I just wanted to. My friend Kim, though, she ran. Of course, she was only nine at the time. She never made it out of her neighbors' yard." And then she told them the story as Kim had told it to her, sitting at her kitchen table, smoking cigarettes and drinking Valpolicella: how she'd run away from home as a little kid, planning to hitchhike from Tampa to New York because her best friend's big sister had told them about 3 Days of Peace & Music in White Lake, New York; how she'd hidden in the neighbors' cabana for hours, until her parents found her and dragged her home kicking and shrieking. "Her parents locked her in her bedroom with her Chatty Cathy," Aradhna said, "and she kept pulling the string till they let her out."

"What's a Chatty Cathy?"

"A doll." Aradhna shrugged, not even attempting to explain what a wonder a talking doll had seemed once upon a time. She could see Kim miming pulling the ring in the doll's back, releasing the cord, her singsong voice mimicking the recording: *Hi, I'm Chatty Cathy! Will you play with me? Please change my dress! I'm hungry! Please take me with you! I love you!* Stubbing out her cigarette, reaching for the pack on the table, her deep-throated laugh. 'Drove my parents freaking nuts. They could've taken the doll away, I guess, but instead they let

me out of my room. But I still didn't get to Woodstock. Well, hell
yes I did—twenty years too late.' Because she'd met David at a Bon
Jovi concert in Jersey in '89 and moved in with him the next week
because he'd told her he lived near Yasgur's Farm. 'And that, my dear,'
Kimmy had said, laughing, 'is what comes of hanging onto a dream.
Who the hell knew that wispy beard hid the soul of an accountant?'
And they'd both dissolved into wine-loosened laughter, bonded by
the glue of their mutually miserable marriages.

"She's here too," Faythe said. "Same as my mom. That's probably
why it's no accident you showed up."

"*I* showed up? I'm not the one who drove halfway across the country."

"We all showed up together. Like that time me and Nan met my
mom on I-40? Only now it's you, me, and Ramon."

"What's he got to do with it?" Aradhna said, disliking, even as the
words came out, how she spoke of him as if he weren't here, as if he
couldn't understand English.

"He's the artist," Faythe answered matter-of-factly. "Oh look." To
their right, just above the line of trees, the tip of the moon showed,
only a fingernail paring's worth, but swelling, rising. "We got to work
fast." She jumped to her feet, rattling off some Spanish, and the two
young people hoisted the ladder and set it against the pole. Ramon
shimmied up the rungs, the canvas bag clunking. Within seconds
the wood-scraping sounds began again.

"Where'd you learn to speak Spanish?" Aradhna asked, pushing
herself up from the ground.

"I took it in school, but mostly I got good from talking to Ramon.
I always thought that was weird, how they make us take Spanish in
seventh grade, but they make all the Mexican kids speak English.
Ramon didn't go to school here though, so he don't think his accent's any good. I tell him it's as good as mine." She called up, "Two
minutes, Ramon! ¡Nada más!"

"Two minutes for what?"

"Before the moon's so high that dude in the truck can't help but see us. You got your mandella?"

"Mandala."

"Yeah."

"I had it." Aradhna searched the ground with her feet till she bumped against the leather bag; she bent to pick it up. The moon was halfway above the horizon now, a full one, ruddy as hell, like a blood orange, and she realized the girl was right. In the light of a full moon their silhouettes would stand out against the landscape. Suddenly it seemed very important that Ramon finish those carvings, as if finishing them meant the seasons would turn back to their proper order and the rains would come again in April, not in a toad-strangling deluge in the fall, and the mice would seek shelter from the cold in October and the geese would fly south for the winter and the fireflies would mate in June as they should. Which was ridiculous, of course. If this was the end of the world, no rite in a hayfield was going to fix things, but when Ramon scrambled down the ladder a moment later and stood formally off to one side, and Faythe said, "Go ahead," Aradhna draped the satchel over her shoulder and began to climb.

The fiberglass rungs were cool beneath her palms. At the top she could just make out the two faces carved in the wood between the outstretched wings, but they were faint, indistinct in the moonlight. They seemed small. Maybe that was just in contrast to the giant, primitive features of the dead artists below. Aradhna touched the two masks, running her hands over the carvings, trying to know which one was Kimmy's. They felt the same. "Which one's Kim's?" she called down in a loud whisper.

"*Abajo*," Ramon said.

"The bottom one," Faythe said.

Aradhna touched the lower face. With the tips of her fingers, she lightly traced the bridge of Kimmy's nose, her cheekbones, the laughing mouth. Yes.

"Do my mom too!" Faythe called softly.

Balancing herself against the ladder, Aradhna dug out the sweetgrass and lit it. She lifted the smoldering braid to the four directions. "This is for both of you then." She waved it at the carved faces, leaned forward, trying to bathe her own face in the smoke, trying to visualize how she'd seen it done by the blond pretendians in the sweat lodge in Sedona two years ago, that Vision Quest Weekend she'd paid a thousand dollars to attend with a dozen other spiritual wannabes. She couldn't remember any of the chants. Aradhna waved the sweetgrass in the air, feeling desperate. She started to hum an old hymn, *rock of ages, cleft for me, let me hide myself in thee*. But, no, that was wrong. She stopped. "This is such bullshit," she said. She had nothing to give the dead: no ceremony, no faith, no ritual. "I'm sorry, girlfriend," she whispered.

A chill was settling over the field. The fireflies had vanished. The land was growing lighter. In her mind's eye she saw Kimmy perched on the monument—not the image from the photograph but the memory from the sweltering day itself, Kimmy leaning back on the slab wearing the beads and tie-dye Aradhna had given her for a joke, flashing the peace sign, laughing, motioning at her to hurry up and take the picture. 'Always the hippie wannabe,' she'd called out. 'Never the freak!' Aradhna had snapped the picture, and at once Kimmy jumped up to stand on the monument, jammed an invisible mic to her mouth, and wailed out a perfect throat-scraping, hair-flinging Janis Joplin imitation: *whoa ah whoa ah whoa!*

Oh God. Her heart hurt.

With her free hand she reached down to run her fingers over the mandala on the leather satchel. Kim had beaded it for her the month before she died—a Christmas present she hadn't lived long enough to give. David had found the package in Kimmy's closet with Aradhna's name on the gift tag last summer when he was clearing out their house for the sale; he'd stopped by to give it to her on his way down to the city. He had called her three times that week, asked her to dinner the next Sunday, a lonely man, bewildered. She'd gone out with him the first time only because she felt sorry for him; that was what she'd told herself, never admitting that she'd been just as lonely, just as lost. *Searching for satellite signal.* Well, it wasn't him. Not David. Not Jerry. Not even these kids. What is it then? Where am I going?

She felt a mantle of warmth wrap around her, and suddenly Kimmy was there with her: she heard Kim's throaty laugh, she could smell her cigarettes. Aradhna clung to the ladder, trembling, the moon yolk-yellow now, swimming huge above the rim of earth, flooding the long sweep of lawn, and she knew she stood out in clear relief, they all did, and it didn't matter, everything was fine, it was fine, it was all going to be all right; and of course she wasn't going to marry David, or move to a vowel state, or go to Canada with these kids, although, yes, she will see them safe to the border. She will do that much. Then she'll return to her half-finished house and spend the winter here in the cold Catskill Mountains. When the snowstorms come barreling down from the north, she will welcome them. She'll build fires in the woodstove. And when spring comes again—if it comes—she will call her brother in Oklahoma, tell him she's on her way home.

Best known for her American Book Award-winning novel about the 1921 Tulsa Race Massacre, *Fire in Beulah*, Rilla Askew has long been telling hidden Oklahoma stories. She's the author of five novels, a book of short fiction, and a collection of creative nonfiction. She's a PEN/Faulkner finalist, recipient of the Western Heritage Award, Oklahoma Book Award, Violet Crown Award from the Writers League of Texas, and a 2009 Arts and Letters Award from the American Academy of Arts and Letters.